She's the Worst

Also by Lauren Spieller

Your Destination Is on the Left

She's the Worst

the

Worst

lauren spieller

SIMON & SCHUSTER BFYR

New York • London • Toronto • Sydney • New Delhi

SIMON & SCHUSTER BFYR

An imprint of Simon & Schuster Children's Publishing Division
1230 Avenue of the Americas, New York, New York 10020

SIMON & SCHUSTER BFYR is a trademark of Simon & Schuster, Inc.
For information about special discounts for bulk purchases, please contact Simon & Schuster Special Sales at 1-866-506-1949 or business@simonandschuster.com.
The Simon & Schuster Speakers Bureau can bring authors to your live event. For more information or to book an event, contact the Simon & Schuster Speakers Bureau at 1-866-248-3049 or visit our website at www.simonspeakers.com.
Jacket design by Krista Vossen
Interior design by Hilary Zarycky
The text for this book was set in Electra.
Manufactured in the United States of America
First Edition
2 4 6 8 10 9 7 5 3 1
Library of Congress Cataloging-in-Publication Data
Names: Spieller, Lauren.
Title: She's the worst / Lauren Spieller.
Other titles: She is the worst
Description: First edition. | New York : Simon & Schuster Books for Young Readers, [2019] | Summary: Told in two voices, sisters April, age sixteen, and Jenn, eighteen, have twenty-four hours to fulfill a childhood pact and deal with a secret that threatens to tear them apart.
Identifiers: LCCN 2018058780 | ISBN 9781534436589 (hardcover : alk. paper) | ISBN 9781534436602 (eBook)
Subjects: | CYAC: Sisters—Fiction. | Family problems—Fiction. | Promises—Fiction. | Dating (Social customs)—Fiction. | Los Angeles (Calif.)—Fiction.
Classification: LCC PZ7.1.S71453 She 2019 | DDC [Fic]—dc23
LC record available at https://lccn.loc.gov/2018058780

For Diana, my sister and best friend.
You inspired all of the good parts of Jenn and April
and none of the bad ones.
I love you.

She's
the
Worst

CHAPTER 1

APRIL

The best part of summer mornings is that I can skip them.

During the school year, I'm up by five to beat my sister to the shower. If I wake up even a few minutes late, I end up hopping from one foot to the other, desperate to use the bathroom, while Jenn straightens her dark brown hair one section at a time. And forget breakfast. I'd rather miss it entirely than hear her tell me for the hundredth time that powdered sugar donuts aren't "brain food."

That's why summer mornings are the best. By the time I roll out of bed, Jenn's reading in her bedroom, her perfectly straightened hair pulled into her signature *Why, yes, I am the valedictorian, why do you ask?* ponytail. I don't have to fight for the shower, or fast until lunch. Instead, I can stand barefoot in the kitchen, my brown curls a bird's nest on top of my head, eating sugary cereal out of a coffee mug, just like I'm doing now. It's perfect.

The other best part of summer mornings is Nate.

"You're up early," he says as he strolls into our kitchen through the back door. He's been coming over, no invitation necessary, since we moved in when I was ten. I remember the first time he appeared in the doorway and took a seat at the table. *I'm Nate Lee. I live next door. Can I have a waffle?*

"It's not early," I say, looking at my cell phone. "It's nine forty-five."

"That's early for you." He grabs a banana and pours himself a cup of coffee, which he promptly puts in the microwave. He's been here often enough to know it's been cold for hours. "Want?" he says, nodding to the pot.

I wrinkle my nose. I've complained about Mom's coffee a million times, but he always asks me anyway. "You realize you don't have to be hospitable in someone else's house, right?"

The timer goes off on the microwave. I pull out the mug and hand it to him.

He takes a sip. "One of these days you're going to say 'yes.'"

"One of these days," I say, "I'm going to lock the back door."

A male voice floats down from the second floor.

"Is your dad still home?" Nate asks.

"Umm . . . no." I fidget with the microwave door, swinging it back and forth. "That's Eric. He slept over."

Nate raises his eyebrows, but doesn't say anything. I get why he's surprised—Eric and I have only been hooking up since the soccer boot camp we both attended at the beginning of summer. But things are already pretty serious between us. He's snuck in my bedroom window a few times already, and last night he stayed over for the first time. Actually, we fell asleep accidentally, but when we woke up at five this morning in a tangle of sheets, he chose to lock my bedroom door and stay until my parents left for the day instead of sneaking back out the way he came in. Which I think says something. I hope it does, anyway.

The floorboards overhead creak, and Eric comes pounding down the stairs, a pair of grassy soccer cleats in one hand and his soccer bag in the other. "There you are," he says. "I was looking for you."

"I hope I didn't wake you up," I say as he comes into the kitchen. "I tried to be quiet."

"No worries," he says, pausing to kiss me on the cheek on his way to the coffeepot. He drops his stuff in the corner, then pours himself a cup and takes a sip . . . and spits it back out. "This is cold. And very bad."

I give Nate an *I told you so* look, but he's too busy frowning down at his phone to notice it.

"What's up, man?" Eric asks him. "You look like someone just stole your high score on Candy Crush."

Nate scowls but doesn't look up. "No one plays Candy Crush anymore."

"My mom does," Eric says. "Or maybe it's FarmVille." He starts to lift the coffee cup to his mouth, then realizes what he's doing and dumps the whole thing into the sink.

"I've got to go. I'm meeting the guys at the field to practice. Gotta look like a stud for that USC rep. He's eyeing me for next fall, and there might even be some scholarship money in it."

He wraps his arm around my waist and pulls me in for a kiss, but I'm too busy fighting off nerves at the mention of the soccer rep to kiss him back. Nobody knows this—not Eric, not my family, not even Nate—but last week, Coach Keisha said my name came up too, and that if I play my cards right, I might be able to get a full ride to USC. I almost died right then and there, because while my grades aren't bad, they aren't impressive either—mostly in the B range, along with an A in Geometry and a C+ in World History. I might get into a few schools, but nowhere like USC. Not with how competitive college is. But with an athletic scholarship? All I'd have to do is maintain my GPA—okay, maybe I'd need to improve it a *little*—and continue kicking ass on the field, and I'd be set.

"You okay?" Nate asks from across the kitchen.

"Yeah," I say, shaking free of my daydream. "Totally."

Eric looks back and forth between us. "Did I miss something?"

"Nope," I say, forcing a smile. "You coming over tonight?"

"If you're lucky." He winks, then slings his soccer bag over one shoulder and nods to Nate. "See you around, man."

Nate looks back down at his phone and grunts.

Eric heads out the back door, leaving Nate and me alone in the kitchen.

"What's wrong with you?" I ask the moment the door

closes. "Why do you get so weird and quiet whenever Eric is around?"

"I just don't like him," Nate says, still not looking at me. "He's a total bro."

"Eric isn't a *bro*. You just don't like athletes."

Nate finally looks up. "I like you," he says, "and you're an athlete."

"Fine," I say, "then you don't like *male* athletes."

"Mike is a male athlete, and he's practically my best friend."

"First of all, Mike is on the bowling team, and the jury is still out on whether that counts as a sport. And second, Mike is *not* your best friend. I am."

"Exactly," Nate says. "You're my best friend, and I'm yours. Which is why it's my duty to be honest with you when I think people are bros. And that guy? He's a *total* bro."

Nate's phone buzzes in his hand, and he looks down again.

"Who keeps texting you?" I ask, nodding to his cell phone.

"My mom."

He frowns again, and it occurs to me that maybe Eric isn't the only reason he's been quiet for the last few minutes. "Is she okay?" I ask. Mrs. Lee is one of the nicest people in our neighborhood, and the idea that something might be wrong with her makes me feel terrible.

"She's fine," Nate says, and puts his phone back in his pocket. "It's no big deal."

"If it's no big deal, then why—"

The stairs creak again, cutting me off. "April?" Jenn calls. "Is there any coffee left?"

"Yeah," I call back, "but it's disgusting."

She takes a step down, and the hem of her plaid pajama pants and her slipper-clad foot comes into view. "Wait—is Nate here?"

He grins. "Good morning, Jennifer."

"Oh," she says. "Be right back."

Her feet disappear, and Nate and I turn to one another. "I'll bet you ten bucks that when she comes down, she's fully dressed and wearing heels," Nate says.

"No way. Heels aren't practical. Keep up."

Jenn reappears a few minutes later. She is indeed fully dressed—she'd never let a non–family member see her in pajamas—and her slippers have been replaced with black leather flats, not heels. Nate tips his head at me in acknowledgment, but I barely notice. Something isn't right. Jenn and I haven't been close in a long time, but I can still read the warning signs. First of all, her hair still looks like mine—a frizzy, curly mess—and second, she's chewing on her bottom lip the way she always does when she's upset.

"Hey," I say. "You okay?"

Jenn pours herself a cup of coffee and puts it in the microwave. "I just have a lot going on."

Jenn *always* has a lot going on. She spent her entire summer hurrying between our parents' antique store in Hollywood, where she clocks as many *I'm the Better Daughter* hours as humanly possible, and her boyfriend's house. But this is the first time she's ever looked anything other than completely presentable and on top of things.

"Is this about Thomas?" I ask her. "He leaves for Stanford in two days, right?"

The microwave beeps, and Jenn takes out her mug. "Kind of."

"It's *kind of* about Thomas," Nate asks, "or he *kind of* leaves in two days?"

Jenn's eyes flash with irritation, but then she sags back against the kitchen counter and sighs. "It's complicated."

Once upon a time I would have pressed her for more, but there's no point these days. If she's going to open up to someone, it won't be me.

Jenn's cell phone rings in the back pocket of her jeans. "Hi," she says. "Are you here?"

There's a low voice on the other end—Thomas. Speak of the khaki-clad devil.

Jenn nods. "Okay, come around to the back and I'll let you in."

"Why does he even bother calling?" I ask after she's hung up. "Why not just come inside like a normal person?"

"*Some* people have manners and don't let themselves into other people's homes," she says, then immediately cringes. "Sorry," she says to Nate. "I didn't mean you."

There's a knock on the back door, and we all turn to see Thomas standing on the other side, waiting patiently to be let in.

"For god's sake," I say, "he knows it's unlocked, right?"

Vampire, Nate mouths to me. *Has to be invited in.*

Jenn glares at us and opens the door.

"Morning," Thomas says, stepping into the kitchen. His hair is neatly gelled, and he's wearing a light blue polo and khakis. He looks like Captain America on his day off, if the Cap wore loafers.

Thomas gives Jenn a quick kiss, then turns to Nate and me. "How is everyone?"

"Not as good as you," Nate says. "You look like you're about to buy a yacht. Or three."

"Or like he's going to explain mortgage-backed securities," I say. "Either one."

"I wish," Thomas says seriously. "The housing market is super lucrative these days."

He hesitates for a second then says, "Come on, guys. I'm *kidding.*"

"Oh, thank god," Nate says. "Because I had no idea what you were talking about."

Jenn links her arm in Thomas's and leans her head on his shoulder. "So what's up?" she asks. "You sounded serious on the phone."

"Um, yeah," Thomas says, his smile gone. "How long till you have to leave for work?"

She checks her phone. "Five minutes?"

"Cool. Can we talk for a sec?"

Jenn glances at me, then leads him out of the kitchen, like she doesn't want me to hear what they're talking about.

Rookie mistake.

When they're gone, I cross the kitchen and press my ear against the swinging door to the living room.

"What are you doing?" Nate asks.

I hold up my finger to shush him, and listen. Jenn's voice is muffled, but I can make out most of what she's saying.

"Tom, I told you—"

"You're going to piss her off," Nate warns. I shush him again, and concentrate on their voices.

"I know, okay?" Jenn is saying. "Stop bothering me about it!"

Whoa. Jenn getting mad at Thomas? Unheard-of.

"I'm just trying to help," Thomas says. "Just promise me you'll tell them today, okay?"

"I will," she says. "I promise."

I step back and grab a random dish towel just as the door swings open. Jenn's gaze travels from my face down to the towel and then back up again. She scowls. "You were listening."

"No, I wasn't."

"Yes, you were," she says, grabbing the towel out of my hands. "You know how I know? Because you *never* clean up after yourself."

Nate laughs, and I stick my tongue out at him.

"Maybe I was listening," I tell Jenn, "but it's only because you were being so sneaky." When she doesn't stop glaring at me, I add, "I could barely hear anyway."

"Good." She folds the towel and puts it back on the counter. Behind her, Thomas looks uncomfortable.

"I'm taking the Prius and going to the store," Jenn tells me. "Nate, are you coming in this afternoon?"

He nods, but doesn't look happy about it. I don't blame him. For the last year he's been working at our family antique store with Jenn. I told him not to—that place is dusty and creepy and totally boring—but he needed a part-time job, and Jenn decided the antique store was perfect for him. And Jenn . . . let's just say she has a way of getting people to do what she wants. Well, most people. I am proudly immune to my big sister's power trips.

"Don't be late," she says. "I have to leave at three."

Nate salutes her. "Yes, ma'am."

Jenn grabs her purse and keys off the hook by the door, and she and Thomas head out, hand in hand.

I hop up onto the counter. "Something's up. She and Thomas were arguing."

Nate quirks an eyebrow. "His-and-hers arguing on the penultimate day of summer before they begin a long-distance romance for the ages? Say it ain't so."

"Do you hear yourself when you talk?" I ask. "Like, really *hear* yourself?"

Nate joins me on the counter. Our legs press up against each other, his thigh warming mine. For a split second, I wonder what would happen if I were to lean into him— then he pulls away. I feel a flicker of disappointment, but I remember the way Eric kissed me last night, the way his body felt next to mine as we fell back asleep, and the feeling disappears. Nate's great, but he's just my friend. Eric is . . .

a lot of things. Captain of the boys' varsity soccer team. Tall and blond and hot in a way that makes me nervous. I'm also pretty sure he's getting ready to ask me to be his girlfriend. Especially after last night.

"What were they arguing about?" Nate asks.

"Who?"

"Jenn and Thomas?"

"Oh! I couldn't hear everything, but she has to tell someone . . . something."

"Very mysterious." He looks over at me, and his smile fades. "Hey, are you actually worried about her?"

I shrug. "Arguing with him isn't like her. I think she might be upset because he's leaving for Stanford in two days and she's staying behind."

"Oh," he says. "That's not funny, then. That sucks."

"Yeah."

"And you still don't know why she isn't going with him?"

"Nope. I've asked a million times, but she insists turning Stanford down was the right decision. She wants to stay closer to home and work at the store."

Which makes *zero* sense. But then again, I've gotten used to not understanding my sister. I didn't know she got into Stanford until I found the acceptance letter in the bathroom trash. If it had been me, it would have been impossible to find someone who *didn't* know I'd gotten in. But that's Jenn. She never brags, never complains, never makes waves, and if I'm being totally honest . . . she's a *teensy* bit boring. But she's also our family's rock. If Jenn's starting to unravel, then there's no hope for the rest of us.

I tap my foot against Nate's. "Maybe we should do something to cheer her up."

"Like what?"

"I don't know—hang out with her? Keep her mind off Thomas leaving?"

"You could come hang out with me at the store." I give him a look, and he sighs. "It was worth a try. Okay, new approach. What makes her happy? What does she like?"

"School," I say immediately. "And antiques. And Thomas."

"Anything else?"

I rack my brain, but Jenn doesn't have hobbies. She doesn't play sports. She has friends, but they're all into the same thing she is: taking over the world one AP class at a time. "Not that I know of."

"Man, that's depressing." Nate rubs the back of his neck. "Okay. She's upset because Thomas is leaving and she's staying here, right?"

"I think so."

"Then maybe you should make her feel better about *that*. Staying here, I mean. I don't know how you make her feel better about Thomas. That's above my pay grade as a neighbor *and* fellow antique store employee."

It's a lame joke, but he's got a point. When Jenn first got into Stanford, she was excited about leaving LA. She might have decided not to go, but she's been dreaming about going away to college forever. And for Jenn, that's a *literal* forever.

She's been talking about this since we were kids. Ever since—

I turn to Nate. "The pact! I forgot all about it."

"So did I, apparently, because I have no idea what you're talking about."

"I doubt I ever told you. It was kind of a secret." I hop down off the counter and start to pace the kitchen. I can't believe I forgot about this. "It was the summer before seventh grade and—"

"Seventh grade," Nate interrupts, a dreamy look on his face. "That was the year I had homeroom with Miss Coppola. But she let us call her Genevieve." He smiles. "I was totally in love with her."

"Are you done?" I ask.

"Yes, sorry. You were in the middle of a precious childhood memory?"

"Right. I was going into seventh grade—which was apparently *super* formative for you, thanks to *Genevieve*—and Jenn was starting high school. She was nervous about it, though, so I took her on this fun, all-day adventure around our neighborhood. It was like we were the Boxcar Children, except instead of collecting teacups and trying to be civilized despite living in a train or whatever, we were eating ice cream and hanging out under the slide at that park down the street. But after a while we got tired, so we went back home and snuck onto the roof of our building."

"You *rebels*," Nate says. "Then what happened?"

"Jenn started talking about how she wanted to go away to college even though she'd only just graduated from middle school. Back then she wanted to go to Michigan or Illinois or something, which I remember thinking was *really* far. Like, why not go to Antarctica while you're at it? But then she got really serious all of a sudden, and said we should promise each other that in four years, when she was leaving for college, we'd spend the entire day together. Just us. To, you know, say goodbye. So we did a pinkie swear . . . and that was it." I wrinkle my nose. "Her fingers were still covered in dry strawberry ice cream, so it was kind of sticky."

"Gross," Nate says. "But also perfect! You can hang out with her tomorrow and fulfill your weird urban adventure pact. I don't know if you'll still fit under the slide, but—"

"No."

"You're right, the slide is really low—"

"No, I mean *no*. We can't."

"Why not?"

"Because there's no way Jenn's going to want to hang out with *me* all day."

Nate's eyes narrow in that particular way they always do right before he tells me not to neg myself. But I know I'm right—I might think my sister is a little boring, but that's nothing compared to the way my sister feels about *me*. I'm pretty sure every time she hears my name, the words "irresponsible," "immature," and "lazy" flash before her eyes. Regardless of how she felt about me back then, Jenn hasn't wanted to hang out, just the two of us, in years. "Besides," I continue, "she's not going away to college anymore. She's staying here. In this city. In this *house*." I jump back up on the counter next to him. "So there's no point."

"Sure there is," Nate says. "The *point* is to take her mind off Thomas leaving, and cheer her up about staying in LA. The pact is just an excuse. A cover story, if you will."

"But a full day is so *long*. And we're older now. We can't just hang out on the playground all day doing nothing."

"Stoner Larry does."

I laugh. "Touché."

"You've just got to come up with a list of her favorite LA things and do all of them. Go to places she likes."

"That would be great if I knew any of that stuff. But I don't." I flick a stray Cheerio across the counter and into the sink. "Okay, what if I put together a bunch of famous LA landmarks instead? Like the Magic Castle and Grauman's Chinese Theatre, or the Hollywood sign? That would be super fun!"

Nate looks unimpressed. "That sounds kinda touristy."

"Yeah," I say, my excitement deflating. "You're right."

"You need to choose places that matter to both of you. That remind you of each other."

"I don't know if you've noticed, but Jenn and I aren't exactly close anymore. The last time we did anything just the two of us was months ago, when we had to pick up that set of dining chairs for Mom and Dad. Not exactly the kind of thing you want to re-create to cheer someone up."

We settle back into silence, both of us thinking, but then Nate slides off the counter. "I'm heading out."

"Wait, you're leaving? I thought you were helping me brainstorm!"

He opens the back door and squints into the midmorning sunlight. "This is about you and Jenn. You're not gonna figure it out if I'm here distracting you." He grabs a banana out of the fruit basket. "Besides, I've only got a few more hours until work. I'm not about to spend them cooped up in here with *you*."

I grab the towel Jenn carefully folded and throw it at him. He catches it and tosses it back on the counter. "See you later?"

"Obviously," I say. "Bye."

Nate leaves, and I pick up my phone. I'm halfway finished typing "Things to Do in LA" into the search engine when I sigh and put the phone back down. Nate's right. If I'm going to make Jenn feel better, I'm going to have to come up with stuff that really matters to her. Stuff *besides* school.

I head into the living room, where we keep all our old family photos.

Time to take a trip down memory lane.

CHAPTER 2

JENN

romise me you'll tell them.

I linger on the sidewalk outside O'Farrell Antiques, Tom's words echoing in my head. I know he's right—he's *always* right. It's the worst thing about him. But just because he's right doesn't mean I'm eager to take his advice. An ambulance flies by, the loud sirens making me flinch. I take one last look at the sunny sky, breathe in the traffic and the pizza shop next door, then push the door open. Or, I try to, because of course—of *course*—it's locked. I groan and pull out my keys. Did I really think Mom and Dad were going to be on time?

I unlock the door and go inside. "Hello, Silvester," I say, patting the small brass statue of a horse that sits on a marble-topped incised walnut side table from 1880 next to the front door. "Did you keep the place safe for me?"

I wander deeper into the store, through the dark rows of furniture and tchotchkes. Dust floats in the light filtering in from the front window, and for a moment I'm suspended in it, like a figure in an old snow globe.

Then I sneeze.

"Oops," I say as I bump into a nearby armchair, knocking over the smiling porcelain clown seated on top in the process. I pick up the doll and turn it over. $700? That must be a mistake. I carry it to the register and lay it gently on the counter. The porcelain monstrosity grins up at me. I turn it facedown. "Creep."

While I wait for my mom's laptop to power up, I turn on lights. Chandeliers, Tiffany lamps, and wall sconces flare to life, filling the room with their warm, inviting glow. Or that's the idea. I think it's a bit much, personally. I also take a moment to organize a shelf of old toys and relocate an antique teddy bear to the steamer trunk that once sat in April's bedroom. Until she complained that our WWII family heirloom was haunted and had to go, that is.

When I return to the counter, the laptop is on. I log in, and a few clicks later the inventory list appears. I scroll down to the toy section, then search alphabetically for "clown." As I suspected, the price is wrong. The doll should be $70, not $700. I take out a pen, prepared to cover one of the zeroes, but then I catch sight of the doll again. The clown has been here for over a year. It's never going to move at that price. And, more important, I hate it. I put the pen down and pull out the price stickers instead.

"How about $60?" I ask the clown's back. "Do you think that's low enough to make someone take you home?"

I turn him over, and he leers up at me.

"You're right. Better make it forty." I write the price on the sticker, then place it on the bottom of his porcelain foot, obscuring most of the previous price—but not all of it. People love markdowns. It makes them feel clever, like they're getting away with something.

That done, I move the clown to the front of the store, where kids will be more likely to find it. Whether they break it or buy it, that thing is going home in the next two days if I have anything to say about it.

I'm on my way back to the counter when the front door opens behind me.

"Don't talk to me like that," Mom is saying. "You always use that tone whenever I—"

She catches sight of me and smiles. "Oh good, you're here."

I breathe through my nose and resist pointing out that without me, the store wouldn't have opened on time.

Dad closes the door behind them. "Jenn, settle something for us. I was just telling your mother—"

"Did you go to the bank?" I ask, interrupting him. I learned years ago that the best way to get them to stop arguing is to shut the fight down good and early.

"Err . . . no," Dad says. "We stopped by the flea market and got distracted."

Of course they did.

Every Friday morning they deposit the cash from the week. Or at least, that's the plan. Usually, there's not much—

most customers pay with credit cards—but occasionally we'll get a big purchase, paid all in cash. Last week someone bought a nineteenth-century armoire for two thousand dollars, and he paid in hundred-dollar bills. It was cool to count it all, but I'm nervous about keeping that much money around for long, especially now that the store's alarm system is broken.

"Maybe you could make the deposit after your shift ends?" Dad asks.

"Stop pushing her," Mom says, coming to stand by me. She rests her hand on my shoulder. "She's got her own life, and you can't expect her to do everything for you."

"I don't expect that," Dad says. "I'm just saying that she could stop on the way home!"

I rub my temples. I can already feel a headache coming on.

Dad crosses his arms—a sure sign that things are about to get worse. If I don't cut this argument off now, it'll go on for at least another ten minutes. "Mom, it's fine. I'll go."

But she's not listening to me. Neither of them are.

"It's not her *job*," Mom says, her hand tightening on my shoulder. "You're always trying to *push* people—"

"I am not."

I curl my fingers into fists, taking a small amount of relief from the way my fingernails bite into my palms.

The front door opens, and a woman steps inside.

Thank god.

"Welcome to O'Farrell Antiques," I say, my voice loud and cheerful. "How can I help you?"

The woman eyes my parents, who, despite her arrival, are still arguing. As if on cue, Mom stomps her foot and says, "That's not what I said and you know it!"

"Um," the woman says, slowly backing toward the door, "maybe I should come back later."

I look to my parents, hoping they'll step in and act like adults for once, but they're oblivious to the fact that they're driving their own customers away. As usual, it's up to me to keep this place functioning.

"If you leave now," I say loudly, "you'll miss our flash sale."

My parents finally go silent.

"For the next hour," I continue, "everything in the store is . . ."

I glance at my dad. His eyes are wide with horror. I turn back to the customer and smile. "Fifty percent off."

Serves them right.

"Oh!" The woman says. "In that case, do you have any Tiffany lamps?"

"Absolutely," I say, careful not to make eye contact with either of my parents. "Follow me."

The woman leaves twenty minutes later, the proud owner of two blue Tiffany lamps and one terrifying clown doll. The moment the door closes, I pick up the dog-eared copy of *Harry Potter and the Goblet of Fire* that April and I share, and turn to the place I left off last night. When summer first started, I vowed to read one book per week so my brain wouldn't turn to mush. My plan was to prioritize the kinds of books you see on those "100 Books to Read Before You Die" lists. That way, I'd be ahead of the curve when classes started in the fall. But after two months of working my way through the collected works of Shakespeare, James Joyce's *Dubliners*, *A Room of One's Own*, and a collection of poems by Langston Hughes, I decided to reward myself with a reread of Harry Potter.

I've barely started to read, however, when my dad storms up to the counter, followed closely by my mom.

"Jennifer, we never take off more than thirty percent!" he says. "You know that."

"Those lamps were worth twice what she paid," Mom agrees.

I put the book down—careful to mark my place—and turn to my parents. "We weren't going to make *any* money if I didn't do something drastic. You would have noticed that if you weren't so busy arguing."

Dad waves this off and wanders into the back room, leaving Mom and me alone. She slips on a dust glove and begins to gently wipe down the various baubles and breakables on the shelf behind the counter. Sometimes I forget she was an art history professor when I was little, back before we moved to Culver City. But when I watch her handle our antiques like they're pieces of priceless art instead of random junk she rescued from estate sales and hotels selling off their old decor in favor of more modern furnishings, it all comes back to me. The endless museum visits, during which Mom would quiz us on Brunelleschi's use of perspective and the properties of illuminated manuscripts as we took yet *another* lap around the Getty Museum. The late nights she spent poring over academic journals while I read Babysitter's Club books to April at her feet. She and Dad had been busy—it turns out being a professor requires a *lot* of late-night grading, and Dad's midlevel management job at a downtown investment bank required him to be at the office at least sixty hours a week—but our parents always made time for April and me. And for each other.

Then when I was in seventh grade, everything changed. Mom and Dad quit their jobs and moved our family to Culver City, where they opened the store. Suddenly, work came first, and instead of spending dinner talking about English tests and the goofy things Dad's boss said at their morning meeting, April and I ate in silence as they flipped through spreadsheets and discussed how to price the mahogany sarcophagus they were having imported from Egypt. By the end of seventh grade, they'd stopped talking entirely—to us and to each other—and started fighting instead. I guess that's what happens when you spend every hour of the day together. You forget you ever liked the other person in the first place.

I try not to compare our lives now to how different things used to be, though. What's the point?

"What are you and Thomas up to tonight?" Mom asks, turning away from the shelves. "Doing anything fun?"

"Just dinner."

"That sounds nice. The two of you are so cute together."

I smile, but then remember the conversation we had this

morning in the living room, and the warm feeling that usually accompanies any mention of Tom disappears. I promised him I'd talk to my parents today, and I meant it. But right now, no one is glaring at anybody else, or arguing about who-knows-what. It's just Mom, silently dusting crystal elephants and hand-blown paperweights, and me. It seems a shame to ruin the peace and quiet. But Tom is right. Now's the time.

I glance at the door my dad just disappeared through, and make up my mind. I'll tell Mom first, and Dad after. That way they can't gang up on me. And then tonight . . . tonight, I'll tell April.

"I'd like to talk to you about something," I say carefully.

Mom puts down the Waterford vase she's holding. "What's up, Jelly Belly?"

I narrow my eyes at the nickname, but say nothing. I gave up trying to get them to stop calling me that a long time ago. I know a lost cause when I see one.

"Hey," she says, cupping her hands around my face. "Is everything okay? You look nervous."

I take a deep breath, readying myself for the confession I've been rehearsing for months—and catch sight of Dad, standing in the doorway, his normally pale face flushed.

"Emma, did you really think I wouldn't find out?"

Mom sighs. "Find out *what*, John? Be specific."

Dad holds up a long, handwritten receipt. "That you *sold* the Steinway?"

I gasp—I can't help it. For months Mom has been threatening to get rid of the grand piano Dad won at auction. At first it seemed like it was going to be a great acquisition, but it turned out to be incurably out of tune, and one of the legs is wobbly. None of this would have been the end of the world—sometimes that's how auctions go—but Dad promised he was going to resell it right away so they could get at least a little bit of their investment back.

That was a year ago.

Mom puts her hands on her hips. "I wasn't hiding it. That receipt has been on your desk for weeks. If you'd ever bother to organize your side of the office, you'd have seen it."

Dad's face goes even redder. "You sold it *weeks* ago?"

"You're lucky I waited that long!" Mom says. "It's been taking up space in the storage unit for almost a year, and you *never* got it appraised like you said you would, so I did it myself."

"Unbelievable," Dad says, shaking his head. "I bet you used that idiot Paul Vega to do the valuation, didn't you?" He crumples the receipt in his hand and throws it on the register. "That man doesn't know a Steinway from a Stairmaster!"

"You're overreacting," Mom says.

"Or maybe I'm just sick of you constantly undermining me," Dad shoots back. "You ever think of that?"

"It's the only way to get anything done!"

"*Stop*," I say loudly, before they can continue. They've had this argument a million times, and it never goes anywhere good from here. "Mom, you should have talked to Dad before you sold the piano. Dad, you should have sold the piano when you said you were going to, or at least talked to Mom about why you didn't do it."

I step between them and lower my voice. I've got their attention. Now I've just got to shut this thing down before they start up again.

"But it's done," I continue. "And the good news is that now you can go back out and buy a *new* used piano. A better one. And once you do, there's plenty of room in the storage unit for it." I look between the two of them and force a smile. "Right?"

The front door opens again, and a man in a suit comes inside the store. I glance at my parents, hoping they might let this argument go in favor of helping the customer, but they're both still sulking. *Great.*

"Mom, why don't you go check out an estate sale?" I suggest. "I heard Maggie Rosenberg's great-aunt Midge just passed. Weren't you just saying the other day that she has some great stuff in her attic?"

"That's right, I was," Mom says, her face lighting up at the prospect. "She has a midcentury buffet that's practically *begging* to be updated."

"And, Dad," I say, "maybe you can run to the bank after all?" He frowns, and I realize my mistake. Dad's *really* sensitive about people assuming his only contribution to the store has to do with the finances, so he always insists on being involved with the antique sourcing as well. "Or you could go with Mom?" I correct. "Check out what Midge has lying around?"

They eye each other, but in the end their desire to see

antiques wins out, because they head toward the back room, leaving me—and the customer—alone at last. It's only then that I remember I had something to tell them.

Thirty minutes later, the customer leaves, and I collapse into an overstuffed armchair, frustration and relief warring inside me. The truth is, I'm in no hurry to tell them. I'm in no hurry to tell *anyone*. But I've been trying for months to get up the courage, and if I don't do it soon, they'll wake up on Sunday morning . . . and it'll be too late.

I pick up a collectible FAO Schwarz teddy bear and hug it to my chest. "Tonight," I whisper to the bear. "I'll do it tonight. No matter what."

CHAPTER 3

APRIL

If someone looked through the living room window right now, they'd probably think I was a conspiracy theorist. I'm surrounded by three notepads covered in messy handwriting, two cardboard boxes, five photo albums, and countless stacks of loose pictures. All I'm missing is a crazed look in my eye and a wall map covered in pushpins and red string. At the very least I look like a scrapbooker with a screw loose.

I pick up the photos I finally settled on, and smile at the picture on top. Jenn and I are sitting next to each other at a picnic table. The sun is shining down on us, and I'm smiling so big you can see the gap I used to have between my teeth, may it rest in peace. Jenn isn't smiling, but her eyes are wide. You can't tell in the picture, but I remember what she was looking at—Dad, standing just outside the frame, holding a sheet cake big enough for twenty people. Jenn was really into the violin back then, so Mom decorated the whole thing with musical notes and instruments and sheet music. Or she tried to. She's not particularly handy in the kitchen, so the whole thing looked a little bit like *Birthday Cake* by Picasso, but it didn't matter. All I cared about was that my big sister wanted to spend her birthday with me instead of her friends.

I press the photos to my chest. When I started looking for inspiration this morning, I thought the whole pact idea was a mistake, and Nate was just being Nate—overly hopeful and incurably encouraging, like a motivational speaker, or a golden retriever. But the longer I flip through these photos, the more I've started to think that maybe this *is* a good idea. Maybe spending the day with Jenn could even be *fun*. We used to love hanging out—we were practically best friends, until she started high school. For the first time in a while, I think maybe we could be again.

A car pulls into the driveway. I know it's Mom and Dad without having to look because their voices carry—up the driveway, through the front door, and into the living room.

"I don't know why you insist on taking Sepulveda," Dad says. "It's always packed."

Mom rolls her eyes. "Like the 405 is any better?"

"If you would just use the Waze app—"

"What is it with you and Waze?" Mom demands. "Are you getting a cut from them or something?" She drops her purse next to the sofa where I'm sitting and looks down at me. "Hi, April."

"Hi. Sorry about the mess. I'm trying to—"

"And besides," Mom says, her attention back on Dad,

"we live five miles from the store. I don't need an app to tell me how to get home."

"It's not about *how* to get home," he says. "It's about the best way to get there."

Mom snorts. "And the difference between those things is . . . ?"

They walk into the kitchen, and I sink back against the base of the couch. Just being in the same room with them makes me tense.

Mom and Dad's argument picks up an octave in the kitchen. I turn on the TV to drown them out, then flip through the rest of the photos I've chosen. As I do, a pit opens up in the bottom of my stomach. What if I'm wrong? What if Jenn doesn't want to do this? What if she doesn't remember the pact, or thinks it's stupid? Or what if she agrees to go, but then we spend the whole day in awkward silence, wishing we hadn't left the house in the first place?

What if she thinks spending the day with me is a waste of time?

Nate's voice sneaks its way into the back of my mind. *Don't assume the worst. This might work out if you give it a chance.* I take a deep breath, and try my best to put my faith in Nate's imaginary advice. Tomorrow is going to be good. Better than good. It's going to be *great*. I'm going to get my sister back. I just have to give her—give *us*—a chance.

"I'm so sick of you *explaining* things to me," Mom says, storming back into the living room. "I told you I wanted to buy the 1940s buffet table, and you said you didn't like it. End of story. No explanation necessary."

"It's not that I didn't *like it*," Dad says, close on her heels. "If you'd stop talking for two seconds and listen to me, you'd understand that."

I don't know how their stupid argument about an app has turned into an argument about a buffet, but I want no part in it, so I turn up the volume on the TV. I normally go to my room as soon as they get home, but I want to be here when Jenn gets back. Otherwise, I might miss her before she goes to bed.

Mom stops next to the fireplace and begins to rearrange the family photos so that Jenn's framed diploma is in the middle instead of my eighth-grade graduation photo. "I'm sick of this conversation," she says. "I don't want to talk anymore."

"Oh, yeah? Well, I'm sick of trying to have a conversation with someone who never listens!" Dad exclaims, raising his voice to be heard over the TV.

"Say something worthwhile and then maybe I'll listen!"

I shuffle through the photos in front of me. I've lost count of how many times I've sat right here, pretending not to hear them bickering back and forth. When I was younger, I tried to help by distracting them with jokes or, when I started playing soccer in middle school, tricks with my ball. One time I even knocked over a vase on purpose, hoping they'd yell at me instead of each other. Anything was better than sitting silently, steeping in their anger. But no matter what I said or did, they'd stare right through me, like I wasn't even there, so I stopped trying.

Their voices continue to climb, so loud I can't even pretend to watch TV anymore. *Screw it.* I might not be able to convince them to play nice, but that doesn't mean I have to sit through this.

"Excuse me?" I call, loud enough to be heard over their shouting. "Are you guys going to keep fighting? Because if so, can you go upstairs?"

"Don't be rude," Mom snaps.

I take a deep breath, and let it out slowly through my nose. *I'm* the one being rude. *Right.*

I dig my fingers into the carpet, and watch Lucy and Ethel's lips move on the TV. If Jenn were here, she'd know exactly what to say to diffuse this situation. She'd probably have them sitting down, working out their differences by the time this episode of *I Love Lucy* is over.

"For the last time," Mom yells, "I don't care about the stupid buffet. Just let it go!"

"This isn't *about* the buffet!" Dad shouts back.

"Then what the hell is it about, John?" Mom demands.

"It's about you never shutting the fuck up!"

They both go completely still. It's as if Dad's words have sucked all the air out of the room, leaving behind nothing but the sound of Lucy's laughter.

They both turn to me at the same time, identical glares on their faces. "For god's sake, April, will you *please* turn that down?" Mom asks. "Your father and I are trying to have a conversation."

I do as she asks, but Dad shakes his head. "Just forget it," he says. "I'm going upstairs."

When he's gone, Mom sinks onto the sofa behind me.

This is the first time we've been alone in weeks, and even though she's my mom, I'm weirdly nervous. "Um . . . are you okay?" I ask.

"I'm fine," she says, shaking her head. "Your father is too sensitive for his own good."

I'm not really sure what to say to that, so I just nod. It must be the right answer, because she smiles, then reaches forward and starts to comb her fingers through my hair. As she separates my curls one by one like she used to do when I was little, all the things I've been keeping bottled up rise to the surface.

Like how I'm worried about how often she and Dad are at each other's throats, but also frustrated because it's not like there's anything I can do about it.

Or that there's this boy, and I might really like him, and I *think* he likes me, but every time those feelings come up in conversation he changes the subject.

But more than anything, I want to tell her about the USC rep that's coming to watch me play when school starts in a few weeks. I know she and Dad don't take my soccer that seriously, but this? *This* they'll have to take seriously. They might even be proud of me. That is, if I ever get up the nerve to tell them.

Mom's hands stop moving suddenly, and my curls fall back into place. "It's a mess in here," she says, looking around the living room. "I don't know what you're doing with these photos, but make sure you clean all this up before you go to bed."

As she stands and walks away, I give myself two long,

deep breaths to feel disappointed. *In. Out. In. Out.* Then I swallow the rest of my feelings and do as she says. I can tell her about soccer later. Or maybe . . . maybe it's better to wait until *after* the USC rep comes. That way, if it doesn't go well, no one will ever know.

I'm putting the last box away in the hall closet when Jenn finally pulls into the driveway. I race to the front door just as it opens.

"Hi," I say.

"Whoa." She takes a step back. "How long have you been standing here?"

"At least three hours."

"Seriously?"

"Of course not." I pull her inside, and close the door. "I've been waiting for you, though. Follow me."

I hurry up the stairs. When I reach the top, I turn to find her still standing at the bottom. "Come *on*," I say.

Without waiting to see if she follows me, I walk across the landing to her bedroom. I sit cross-legged on her bed, but I don't bother getting comfortable. No way she's going to let me spend more than a few minutes in her room alone, anyway. What if I break something, or un-alphabetize her books?

As predicted, Jenn comes into her room seconds later. She sees me sitting on her bed, the ratty quilt grandma gave her beneath me, and looks down at my feet.

"I'm not wearing shoes," I reassure her. "Are you ready?"

Jenn hangs her purse on the back of her door, checks her hair in the mirror, then lowers herself into the ergonomic desk chair Mom and Dad got her for her birthday last year. "Ready for what?"

"This." I reach into my pocket and pull out my cell phone. The Notes app is already open, my glorious plan on display—ten destinations, each one corresponding to the stack of photos I left downstairs on the couch. I hand my phone to her and mentally pat myself on the back for putting this all together *without* Nate's help. Truly, I am the best sister in the entire universe. I am grace and giving and all things good.

But instead of being excited or, I don't know, touched by my generosity and creativity, Jenn just looks confused. "I don't understand what this is."

"What do you mean you 'don't understand'? It's a schedule! See the times along the side?"

"Yes," she says slowly, like I'm an idiot. "I can see that. But I don't know what it's *for*."

Jenn yawns and hands the phone back to me. "April, I've had a long day. I'm tired. Either explain it to me or get out of my room."

"Okay," I say, forcing myself to stay calm even though I want to tell her to stop being such a freaking *adult*. "I noticed you seemed a little sad this morning, and I heard you talking to Thomas—"

"I knew you were listening!"

"Not the point," I say, holding up my hand to silence her. "You seemed upset, and I realized that this whole thing is probably hard on you."

"What 'whole thing'?" she asks.

"This whole staying-in-LA-for-college thing! You're gonna be here, and everyone else is leaving, and that's gotta suck. I mean, it's kinda your fault it's happening. You *could* have just gone to Stanford. . . ."

Jenn narrows her eyes.

"Anyway, that's why I made this list. I know it just looks like a list of locations around LA, but each one corresponds to something that'll remind you of how great it can be to live here." I think of the endless albums I sorted through before settling on the perfect ten photos—the perfect ten memories—and my heart swells. "And, you know, how close we used to be. And maybe . . . how close we can be again."

A funny expression comes over Jenn's face. "You did all this for me? Today?"

I pull one of her three matching throw pillows onto my lap. "I was trying to figure out how to cheer you up, and then I remembered the pact we made, and it all sort of came together." I search her face for signs she knows what I'm talking about, but her face is blank. "Do you remember the pact? You were about to start freshman year, and you said—"

"Yes," she says. "I remember."

I sit back, relieved. "Then you get it? The schedule, I mean."

"I do." Jenn looks down at her perfectly manicured fingernails and takes a long, deep breath. "April, this is so nice. And I truly appreciate it. But . . . it's not a good idea."

My shoulders slump. "Why not?"

"It's . . . complicated. I have to wrap a few things up before school starts, and I need to talk to Mom and Dad—"

I stand up so fast the pillow in my lap falls to the floor. I don't bother picking it up. "I get it. You're too busy to hang out with me. It's fine."

I shove my phone into my back pocket and head for the door, but Jenn blocks my way. "You don't have to go," she says. "We could talk—"

"No need," I say, and push past her.

My room is dark when I enter, but I don't bother turning on the lights before flopping onto my bed. I spent hours planning this stupid day for Jenn, but I should have known it was a waste of time. That she wouldn't see how hard I worked on it. It's been years since we made that pact. Years since she was the kind of person who would enjoy something like this. The kind of person who made goofy faces when I was too scared to sleep, or spent two hours teaching me to play Crazy Eights so I wouldn't be the only one at Monica Bleaver's sleepover who didn't know how. That Jenn doesn't exist anymore, and I was an idiot for thinking otherwise.

I need to talk to someone who will understand. Someone who won't judge me if my voice gets squeaky when I inevitably cry. I grab my phone and start to dial Nate, but stop. If Eric and I are getting serious, we need to start doing more than just hooking up and talking about soccer. Maybe if I'm the one who opens up first, it'll make him feel more comfortable.

I dial Eric and listen as the phone rings. And rings. And rings. I sigh and put my phone aside. I should have known better than to think he'd be free on one of the last nights before school starts.

My phone buzzes next to me. I flip it over, expecting it to be Nate asking how the big reveal went, but instead I find a text from Eric.

You called?

I sit up in bed, my heart pounding in my chest. I don't know why he didn't call me back, but it might be easier to talk about stuff over text anyway.

Yeah, I type back. **I had a fight w/ my sister.**

Three little dots appear, signaling that he's typing back. I wait, my leg bouncing with anticipation. Is he going to ask what happened? Or maybe tell me about his own sister? I've never met her, but I remember seeing her around the halls when I was a freshman and she was a senior. They couldn't have gotten along *all* the time.

The three little dots disappear, then start again. His message arrives seconds later.

That sucks.

I wait for him to say more, but the chat stays blank. *Shit.* Maybe I should say something. Explain more. Or maybe saying something in the first place was a mistake. Things are still pretty new between us. I'm probably getting ahead of myself by expecting him to talk to me about my family. I bet he thinks I'm high maintenance now, and is wondering if Jenn and I have some kind of horrible, bloodthirsty relationship—

Another message arrives, interrupting my anxiety spiral.

Can I come over?

I bite my lip. My parents are downstairs, but if Jenn hears him sneaking in, she'll tell them for sure. Not that they'd care one way or the other what I'm doing. But Jenn would probably still interrupt us in some misguided attempt at "protecting me," like she tried to do a few weeks ago when Eric ran into her in the hallway on his way to the bathroom at two in the morning. Apparently, she did *not* appreciate him wandering around in his boxers.

Can I come to you instead? I ask.

I stare at the screen, waiting for his reply. I've never been to Eric's house, but I know where it is. I may or may not have driven by it three times in the last week.

My phone buzzes again.

Sorry, parents home.

I tap my phone against my leg. Maybe this is an opportunity. He usually comes over here, but that always ends in us hooking up. What we need is a public place where we can talk for real—maybe about Jenn, maybe not—and get to know each other.

Want to take a walk? I ask.

I watch my phone. I want him to say yes, but more than that, I want him to *want* to say yes.

Too tired. 😔

I let my phone slip out of my fingers onto my bed. "Damn it," I whisper into the dark. I knew I was pushing too hard. Asking too much. I should have just kept my sister drama to myself.

Better yet, I never should have offered to spend the day with Jenn in the first place.

CHAPTER 4

JENN

I don't know what surprises me more. That April remembered the pact we made as kids, or that she actually wanted to do it.

I unwrap my nightly moisturizing mask and lay it onto my face, careful to line up the holes for my eyes and nose. I've been using a mask every night for the last year as a way to help quiet my mind before I go to bed. Otherwise, I just lie there, staring up at the ceiling, making to-do lists and listening to my parents argue through the walls.

When the mask is on, I sit cross-legged on my bed and do the second thing that always help me unwind: reading. I'm a few pages into the first task of the Triwizard Tournament when my cell phone buzzes beside me. I don't bother checking the caller ID because it's the same person who's called me every night before bed since we first started dating—Tom. Instead, I put the call on speakerphone and say, "I know what you're going to say, but the answer is *no*."

"Are you *sure?*" Tom asks, his voice amplified. "It might be fun to hang out with your sister for a few hours."

I knew it was a mistake to text him about her offer. He's too softhearted. "I can't," I say, setting Harry Potter aside. "I still haven't finish packing."

"But it's the perfect opportunity to tell her—"

"I know, but spending the whole day with her like that . . . It's not a good idea. We'll argue, and it'll just get out of hand like it always does."

"Why did you made the pact in the first place if you didn't want to do it?"

"At the time, I *did* want to do it. I was fourteen. I didn't know how much things would change between then and now."

Tom is quiet for a moment, long enough that I check my phone to make sure we weren't disconnected. Then he says, "I just think it'd be good for you to spend some time with her. You're always angry at her—"

"Because she's constantly doing things that are completely selfish and unreasonable."

"Maybe this is a good chance to put all that behind you. She said she wants to hang out with you, right?"

I stand back up again and start to pace. "Look, I know this pact thing seems nice, but you don't know April the way I do. At the beginning of summer, I asked if she could cover a shift at the store, and in exchange I did the dishes for a whole week. But then—"

"She didn't show up because she had soccer practice," Tom says. "I know. But that's just one time."

"Oh, yeah? Just last week she told me she wanted to borrow my yellow dress, and when I told her I already had plans to wear it, she immediately asked me if she could borrow my favorite jean jacket instead."

"So?"

"So, I don't think she even wanted the dress—I think it was about the jacket all along!"

Tom sighs. "Don't take this the wrong way, but you sound completely paranoid."

I throw my hands up. I *know* I sound paranoid. But Tom doesn't understand what it's like living with my sister. Nothing is ever straightforward with her. She's always got a motive, and usually it involves getting out of doing something, *especially* when that something involves our parents. When she was younger, I wanted to protect her, but by the time she turned thirteen—the same age *I* was when I began playing interference between my parents—I wasn't just tired of the constant yelling. I was tired of pretending everything was okay. So I stopped.

Unfortunately, it didn't matter. April saw what was going on between them, but instead of stepping up to the plate like I had, she turned her back on the problem entirely. She'd leave the house, or simply turn on the TV so loud that she didn't have to listen to them. I tried to be patient with her, to give her time to adjust. But eventually, I ran out of patience and was forced to accept that she wasn't a baby anymore, too young to handle our parents arguing. She just didn't want to be bothered.

Maybe that's why this whole pact thing rubs me the wrong way. April remembers agreeing to it, but she doesn't remember why we were hanging out that day in the first place. She doesn't remember me finding her curled up in her closet, hiding from the noise. All she cares about is what we did that day—the outing I planned to get her out of the house. Now she's sixteen, and she's still letting me take care of Mom and Dad on my own while she sneaks around with some jock and ignores her responsibilities at home.

"Jenn, I hear you," Tom says. "And maybe you're right. But even if you are, it still might not be the worst thing in the world to get April on your side before you talk to your parents."

I lean over and pick up the pillow April dropped on her way out of my room. "April is never on anyone's side but her own."

The floorboards outside my room creak. "Jenn?" my dad calls softly through the door. "Are you still awake?"

"Tom, I've got to go," I say, taking the call off speakerphone. "My dad needs something."

"Okay. But think about going with her tomorrow, okay?"

His voice sounds so earnest it about breaks my heart. Tom's always cared about my relationship with my family, but I've never heard him be this serious about it before. "If it's this important to you, then yes, I promise I will *think* about it. But that's it."

"Thank you," he says.

"You're welcome. Dinner tomorrow night?"

"Yep. See you at six."

"Got it," I say. "Love you."

I wait for Tom to answer, but the line goes dead. I'd normally call back—he probably just didn't hear me—but my dad knocks again. "I know you're awake in there. I can hear you talking."

I throw my phone on the bed, then cross my room and open the door.

"Yikes," my dad says the moment he sees me.

"What?"

He points to my face and grimaces.

Oh right, the mask. I peel it off. "Happy?"

"Much better."

"Great," I say, smiling tightly. "What's up?"

"Do you know where your mother put the file of tax documents? They aren't in the home office, and I don't remember seeing them at the store."

"Have you asked her?"

He shrugs. "She's not speaking to me."

So much for my face mask helping me relax before bed. "Did you look in the cabinet under the desk?"

"It's not there."

"What about the drawer in the credenza?"

"Nope."

I think for a moment. "What about Mom's old briefcase? The one she stopped using after you spilled orange juice on it. I think it's in the downstairs hall closet next to the vacuum cleaner."

He brightens. "I have *not* looked there."

"Then there you go," I say, starting to close my door. "Good night—"

"Wait," he says, stopping me from closing it. "I want to ask you something else."

I open the door again. "What?"

"Your mother is insisting we go to the bank together tomorrow morning, so we need you to cover the store."

"That wasn't a question," I say, narrowing my eyes. "Dad, I worked the last four days in a row. Tomorrow is my day *off*."

"I have good news for you: working *five* days in a row will be good practice for adulthood," he says, winking.

I groan. "Can't one of you go while the other works? Do you have to go *together*?"

"Take it up with your mother," he says. "Actually, don't. She'll just get pissed at me."

He starts to walk down the hallway, and the urge to shout at him builds inside me, so fast and furious that for once I don't even try to stop it. But instead of yelling at him about how it isn't fair, or how he's going to need to find out someone else to work at the store because my days there are numbered, what comes out of my mouth catches me by surprise.

"I'm hanging out with April!"

He turns around. "What, now?"

"No," I say. "Tomorrow."

I glance at her door, half expecting her to come out and call me a liar, but it stays closed. She must have snuck out or fallen asleep. "She invited me to hang out with her, and I already said yes." I lift my chin and give him the look I see him use on antique dealers when he's trying to convince them he'll walk away if they don't agree to his price. "I can't turn my back on a commitment."

"*Fine,*" he says, shaking his head. "But you need to get Nate to cover your shift."

I want to protest that it's *Dad's* shift that needs covering, but sometimes you've gotta quit while you're ahead. "Will do," I say. "Good night."

"Love you, kid," he says as he walks back down the hall.

My stomach twists. As angry as he and Mom make me, I love them too. "Night, Dad."

I go back into my room and pick up my cell phone. I quickly text Nate, and he immediately agrees to cover for me. Then I text Tom.

You'll be glad to hear I'm hanging with April tmrw. Gonna have a lot to tell you at dinner. 😬

I wait for him to reply, but my phone stays silent. He must have gone to sleep. I finish getting ready, then crawl into bed. It's only then that I realize what I've just agreed to—a full day with my sister, and nothing to distract us besides wherever she decides to take me.

There's no way we'll get through the entire day without arguing. No way. But maybe Tom is right about telling her before I tell my parents. It'll be good practice, and it's not like she's going to care one way or the other. Knowing April, she'll probably listen just long enough to determine whether what I'm saying affects her, then change the subject or ignore me entirely.

I scoot down under the covers and turn off the light.

Good thing I'm used to it.

CHAPTER 5

APRIL

*pril.*

    April.

    APRIL.

"WHAT?"

"Are you awake?" Jenn calls through the door.

"No." I cover my head with my pillow to block the light shining through my window. It's summer. I shouldn't even know what the morning light *looks* like, let alone what it feels like on my face.

"It's time to get up," Jenn says on the other side of the door. "Otherwise, we're going to be late."

I throw the pillow aside. "Late to what?"

There's a weird rattling noise, and a second later my door opens, revealing Jenn in the doorway. "To our Special Sister Day, obviously. Isn't it supposed to start at eight? I thought that's what your schedule said."

"Okay, I never called it that, and you should be embarrassed that you just did." I sit up in bed. "Also, you said you didn't want to go."

Jenn comes inside and sits on the edge of my bed. It's not even seven forty-five and she's already dressed in a J.Crew romper, cardigan, and the same black flats from yesterday.

"I know," she says, "and I'm sorry. You were trying to be nice, and I was . . . not."

I yawn. "No, you really weren't."

"But it's not too late, is it? We could still go?"

I lie back in bed. I want to tell her there's still time, but I'm tired of letting everyone in my family treat me like a nuisance. "Sorry, but I made other plans."

"With who?"

"Nate."

Jenn shakes her head. "I texted him last night. He's covering my shift until Mom and Dad can go in at eleven thirty."

Damn you, Nate. "Fine, I didn't make other plans. But that doesn't mean you can change your mind and expect me to jump out of bed and be ready to go in five minutes."

Jenn frowns. "Why not? Isn't that what you normally do?"

I glare at her, but then her lips twitch, and I realize she's teasing me.

"So are we going or what?" she asks.

The words *I don't want to* are on the tip of my tongue, but I realize they're not actually true. I *want* to go. I do.

"Okay, okay," I say, pushing her off the bed. "Go away so I can get dressed."

Jenn starts toward my door, but stops. "There's just one

thing. I have to be back home by five thirty. I'm getting dinner with—"

"Thomas," I say. "Yeah. I figured."

"Cool. I'll meet you downstairs in fifteen minutes."

"Wait," I say as she turns to leave. "How the hell did you open my door just now? I locked it last night."

She pulls a bobby pin out of her perfectly straightened ponytail. "I used this."

"Seriously? That's actually kind of impressive."

She smirks and sticks it back into her hair. "Maybe I'm not as lame as you think I am."

"Did you learn how to do it on YouTube?" I ask.

"Maybe."

I grin and throw back the covers. "Then you're exactly as lame as I think you are."

When she's gone, I fire off a text to Nate. **Scheming behind my back, huh?**

He sends back a string of winking emojis, plus a dog GIF for good measure. I smile, then toss the phone aside and start to get dressed. We're a little behind schedule, but a bit of old-fashioned aggressive LA driving will help us catch up. Plus, Jenn seems like she's in a good mood, which is lucky, since spending all day together is going to be awkward. We haven't done it since she met Thomas.

I take off my old AYSO soccer jersey, pull on cutoffs and a vintage T-shirt I got on supersale at a boho store on Abbot Kinney, and run a bit of antifrizz serum through my curls.

Then I grab my sunglasses and my purse and head downstairs.

Special Sister Day, coming right up.

Thirty minutes later, Jenn and I are standing in front of our first stop: The Conservatory for Coffee, Tea & Cocoa. The line is so long it stretches out the door and around the corner.

"Wow," Jenn says. "I've never seen it this busy."

I crane my neck to see what the holdup is. We're across the street from Sony Pictures, so it wouldn't surprise me if there's someone famous here. That would explain the crowd—suddenly everyone and their mother needs a latte the second Emma Watson stops by. Unfortunately, it doesn't look like that's the problem; they're just regular old busy.

We get in line. Jenn takes out her phone, probably to text Thomas about how lame this is. I sigh and pull the envelope of photos out of my purse. In the first one, twelve-year-old Jenn and ten-year-old me are sitting inside Conservatory underneath the large, fake tree they keep in the corner, two huge mugs steaming in front of us. We'd moved across town to Culver City two days earlier, and Mom and Dad brought us here to celebrate. Jenn took one look at the massive burlap bags full of coffee beans and the old men doing crossword puzzles out front and immediately fell in love with the place. And since I was still in my *I want to do everything Jenn does* phase, I immediately loved it too. The fact that the hot chocolate was amazing didn't hurt either.

I shove the photos back in my bag. I'd thought Conservatory would be the perfect place to start this day, but by the look of this line, I was wrong.

"Hold on a second," Jenn says. "I'll be right back."

She walks past the line, then disappears inside Conservatory. I don't know what she thinks she's going to accomplish by going in. I sigh and lean against a parking meter. I should have known this place was going to be a madhouse. It's eight thirty a.m. on a weekday and Sony employs roughly ten bajillion people across the street, not to mention all the other businesses in downtown Culver City. This was a stupid idea.

I take out my phone and text Nate. **Conservatory is packed. Need backup plan.**

His reply comes fast, like he was waiting for something like this to happen. **Coffee Bean is nearby.**

Ugh, Coffee Bean. Everyone in LA is all about it, but if there's one thing Jenn and I *do* agree on, it's that Coffee Bean sucks. All the chains do. Maybe that makes me a snob—okay, it totally makes me a snob—but I don't care. Coffee Bean and Starbucks suck. Anyone who disagrees can come at me.

Except this line hasn't moved, and the clock is ticking. We might have to settle. I send Nate a thank-you. It's not his fault Conservatory is the busiest place on the planet.

"Hey."

I look up, and find Jenn holding two ceramic Conservatory travel mugs.

"I got you a mocha," she says. "I hope that's okay."

"How did you—"

"A friend used to date the guy behind the counter. I texted him to see if he was working, and he was." She hands me my drink. "The mochas were free, but I paid for the mugs."

I start to reach for my wallet, but she shakes her head. "They're on me. I figure we can keep them to remember today by, when we're apart."

I take a sip. *Delicious.* "I don't know when we're going to be apart, but that's still really nice. Thank you."

She frowns, and I realize my mistake. The last thing she needs right now is a reminder that she's not going anywhere. "Actually," I say quickly, "I have an idea for how we can remember today, too."

I pull the Conservatory photo out of my purse and hand it to her. "I was thinking we could take a selfie at each place we go. Like a before-and-after thing."

"I hate selfies."

I roll my eyes. "Of course you do."

"Oh, all right. But I'm only doing it if no one is watching. I hate trying to look cute and spontaneous when everyone around me knows I'm faking it."

"Everyone knows because everyone does it," I say. "So there's no point in being embarrassed. But fine—we'll only take super private selfies."

Jenn snorts. "That sounds inappropriate."

I swat at her, almost dropping my drink in the process, then pull out my phone. Jenn leans toward me, and we smile for the camera.

"Say 'cheesy,'" she says.

Click.

One stop down. Nine to go.

The Santa Monica Pier is usually packed with kids during summer, but the day camps must not be here yet because the place is practically empty when we arrive. Jenn and I walk down the pier, past the arcade and the woman selling cotton candy (does anyone actually *eat* cotton candy this early in the morning?), almost all the way to the end. When our destination is directly in front of us, I throw out my arms. "Surprise!"

Jenn looks confused. "The Ferris wheel?"

I try not to let her lack of excitement get to me. "Yes!"

I buy two tickets from a guy in a red-and-white polo, then we get on. Jenn takes a seat on the far side of the car. It's big enough for at least six people, but it feels weird to sit on the other side, so I take a seat right next to her.

"So? What do you think?" I ask.

She folds her hands in her lap and looks over the far side, out at the ocean. "It's a beautiful day."

"Yeah," I say impatiently, "but I mean about the Ferris wheel! Do you remember coming here?"

"Sure do," she answers stiffly.

Why is she being like this? Everything was totally fine, and now she's sulking. What did I do wrong?

The Ferris wheel shudders, and we start to move. A kid in the car above us cheers. I scoot to the other side and look down. We're not moving very fast, but we're already at least five feet in the air above the ride operator's hut. The Ferris wheel continues to climb, and I look farther out, past the roller coaster, past the end of the pier, where a few people are fishing, to the ocean beyond. The morning sun glints off the small, white-capped waves. I breathe in the smell of seawater and sunshine and popcorn, then pull the second photo out of my bag. "Remember this?"

Jenn takes the picture from me. "I was still having fun when this was taken."

"What do you mean?" I ask. "The whole day was fun."

Jenn gives me her patented *Are you serious?* look and holds up the photo. She's almost eight, and I'm six. We're seated on this very Ferris wheel—I can even see the roller coaster in the background. Her hair is short and uneven (this was the year she decided to cut it herself), and I'm missing one of my front teeth. Jenn is holding a half-eaten ice-cream cone, and if the chocolate smeared around my mouth is any indication, I've just finished eating mine. But instead of smiling for the camera, we're whispering to one another, our heads so close together that you can't tell where her brown hair ends and mine begins.

"We rode the Ferris wheel ten times," Jenn says. "Do you remember?"

I think back, and yes, that sounds right. "Dad used up all our tickets on it," I say. "We kept getting back in line."

"Right. But do you remember what happened the *last* time we rode?"

"Um . . . no?"

Jenn crosses her arms. "You threw up."

I laugh. "Really?"

"Yes, really!"

"Huh. I forgot that." I shrug. "I don't get what the big deal is, though."

"What the big—April, you threw up on *me!*"

It all comes back. The hot dog. The double scoop of chocolate ice cream. The Ferris wheel. Going *up, up, up,* and then lurching to a stop. The sudden, unstoppable nausea. And finally, Jenn's face, red and streaming with tears as she stood up, her shirt covered in—

"Oh, no," I whisper.

Jenn sits back, a look of grim satisfaction on her face. "Oh, yes."

I look at the photo again. Our parents must have taken it before our last ride. Before I puked all over my sister.

"You threw up before we were even halfway," Jenn says. "I had to ride the Ferris wheel all the way around three times before it was finally our turn to get off." She shudders. "I can still smell the hot dog."

"Okay, I'm sorry I threw up on you, and I'm sorry I don't remember it. But can we just pretend that didn't happen? For, like, twenty minutes?"

Her phone chimes in her lap. She reads the text, and her shoulders tense.

"Everything okay?" I ask.

She nods.

"You sure?"

"Yeah, I'm just . . . nervous."

"About Thomas leaving?" I ask, nodding at her phone.

"I know it's gonna be weird, but you guys will be okay, right? You've been dating for almost two years, and he's super into you. And it's only an hour flight if you want to visit."

Jenn looks unconvinced, so I pull out the envelope of photos and try another approach. "I know I screwed up with this whole Ferris wheel thing, but we're going to a ton of places you'll like today. Places you'll be able to visit any time you want now that you're staying in LA. Maybe you and I can even do some of them again after school starts. It's not like we need a pact to hang out."

Jenn's face contorts, and for a horrible second I think she's going to cry. Is hanging out with me really that painful? But the expression disappears just as quickly as it came, and when it's gone, she no longer looks sad. She looks determined.

"April, there's something I have to tell you." She takes a deep breath, like she's gathering all her strength. "You know how I got into Stanford, but decided not to go?"

"Yeah?"

"That's not exactly what happened."

I frown. "I don't understand. Did you not actually get in? Why would you lie about that?"

She looks down at her hands. "No, I did get in. But I didn't turn them down."

"Oh," I say, the truth slowly sinking in. "So that means—"

"That I said yes. I'm going."

I stare at her, incredulous. I've wondered for months why someone with straight As and amazing SAT scores would turn down one of the best schools in the country to go to community college instead. The only reason I could come up with—the only reason Jenn ever gave—was that she didn't want to be too far from our parents and the antique store. It never even occurred to me that she might be lying.

"Wait," I say, "do Mom and Dad know?"

Jenn rubs her palms against her knees, pulling the fabric of her romper taut. "Not exactly."

My mouth drops open.

"I'm going to tell them," she says quickly. "I was actually about to tell them yesterday at the store, but then Dad found out Mom sold this piano he bought, and it turned into a whole thing. So I was going to tell them last night instead, but I didn't get the chance."

"*Didn't get the chance?* Jenn, you've known for months!"

"I know. I meant to tell you guys a long time ago, but I was afraid that . . ." She exhales. "I just didn't have a choice, you know?"

"No, I *don't* know. Why did you lie in the first place? Why didn't you just tell them from the beginning? It's not like Mom and Dad told you not to go—"

"You don't know what you're talking about!" she snaps. "I did what I had to do, okay?"

The Ferris wheel comes to a sudden stop. We both look over the edge and watch a small girl climb off at the bottom.

"Please stop pushing," Jenn says when we start moving again. "It's my life, and I've made my decision. I'm going to Stanford."

I lean back in my seat, frustration and confusion warring

inside me. None of this makes any sense. Jenn is the responsible one. She would never do something like this. Never. And yet, here we are.

"How did you even do it?" I ask. "Don't you have to, like, pay up front or something to hold your place? You don't have that much money, do you?"

"Grandma made the down payment," Jenn says, "and I did all the federal loan paperwork myself. It wasn't as hard as it sounds, to be honest. The tricky part was intercepting all the mail before Mom and Dad saw it. Luckily, they almost never remember to check the mailbox anyway."

She laughs, and I realize with a jolt that she's actually *proud* of herself. Is this who Jenn is now? And if so, when did it happen and how the hell didn't I notice?

The Ferris wheel stops again for another kid to climb off. I grip the seat beneath me. I wish this thing would hurry up already. "When do you leave?"

Jenn reaches around for her ponytail and tugs on the end. "That's the tricky thing. . . . I leave tomorrow."

"*Tomorrow?*" I shake my head. "I cannot believe you haven't told them already. I can't believe you didn't tell *me*."

Except I can. Jenn never tells me anything, and I never tell *her* anything either. It's just how things are.

She scoots closer, so our knees are touching. "April, I know you're mad. But this is my last day in LA, and I'm spending it with you. Doing this pact thing. I should have told you the truth sooner, but at least we have today to hang out. Right?"

I look away from her, out at the ocean. I thought today was going to be about cheering up my sad, selfless sister, but instead it turns out she's a jerk who lied to her family for months *and* let me put together this whole entire day under false pretenses. If I thought I felt invisible in my family before, it's *nothing* compared to how I feel now.

"Mom and Dad are going to freak out when you tell them," I say.

"They'll get over it," Jenn says. "They'll have to." Then she gives me a look, as if to say, *And so will you.*

We settle into silence, and I realize we're already on our third rotation of the Ferris wheel. I wish I'd noticed before we started it—I would have pretended there was an emergency so I could get off early.

Jenn must notice me looking down at the ride operator, because she asks, "Do you want to go home?"

"Maybe," I say. "I don't know."

The Ferris wheel continues to climb. I scoot all the way to the end of the seat and look down at the carnival below. Kids have started to show up, all of them dressed in their day camp colors. I watch one little boy throw a baseball into a stack of milk bottles. He misses.

I pick up the envelope in my lap. We have eight more locations to visit. Eight more chances to connect with my sister and make things between us like they used to be.

Suddenly, that feels like way too many.

CHAPTER 6

JENN

That went about as well as could be expected.

The metal gate clangs open, and April is off the ride and striding into the crowd, cell phone in hand, before I've even realized it's time to get off. I'm debating running after her when my phone buzzes in my pocket. I pull it out and see she's sent me a text.

Bathroom. brb.

I look around for somewhere to sit, but every bench is either occupied or covered in sticky ice-cream stains, so instead I wander away from the rides to a quieter part of the pier. I lean over the railing and watch the waves roll in below, crashing against the wooden support beams, filling the air with the smell of briny water and rotting wood. April's always loved the pier—the loud games and bright lights, the smell and taste of salty-sweet carnival food—but I prefer the sound of the ocean.

Our parents took us to the beach all the time when we

were kids, but it was me who introduced April to the water. I had to convince her to wade into the cold Pacific, promising her she'd get used to the temperature. When our goose bumps finally subsided, we'd splash each other and dig our toes into the loose sand, squealing when seaweed wrapped around our ankles. April was always happiest where the water was only waist-deep and our parents could spot us easily from their places farther up the beach. But I was never content to stay where it was safe. I'd swim out, past the couples kissing in the shallows; past the boogie boarders, their eyes trained on the horizon, waiting for the next swell to carry them back to shore. Past even the breaking point, where the waves would force you to either jump above them or dive below.

I'd swim so far out the waves would calm again, and I was alone. Sometimes I'd float on my back, watching the sun-made shapes chase one another around the insides of my eyelids. Other times I'd watch the people on the other side of the breaking waves and pretend that I was a lonely mermaid watching a play put on by the funny humans on the beach. There goes the little boy in blue-and-green trunks, chasing a red ball down the beach. There's the girl in the one-piece, fanning herself with an open paperback book while her boyfriend buys her a soda. And there's April. Playing in the shallows, making castles from the wet sand, lost in a world of her own making while our parents nap together on their bright green beach blanket, big enough for two.

I loved being on the other side of the waves. But I'd never stay out there for long. I'd eventually remember that April wasn't just a kid playing on the beach. She was my sister. And she wasn't building that castle by herself because she wanted to. She was doing it because I wasn't there to help. So I'd swim back in, and together we'd haul wet sand up the beach, each bucketful a precious commodity in our construction. April always wanted to build *up*, to have the tallest castle on the beach. But the thing about castles is that they're only as strong as their defenses. So while she added turret after turret, each one strung with dark green seaweed banners, I'd dig moats and build walls, everything I could to keep the castle safe from the water rushing up the beach.

I know April's mad, but even though she doesn't understand why I did what I did, surely she can see how important this is to me. How badly I need to get away. How *sick* I am of being in charge of everything, how much I hate constantly taking care of Mom and Dad, how sometimes my life here makes me want to *scream*—

I grip the wooden railing, matching my inhales and exhales to the movement of the waves below.

Last night, April said she wanted to be close again, like we were as kids. I didn't believe her, but after seeing how disappointed she was about me moving away, it seems like maybe she was telling the truth. I know this isn't how she pictured today going, but assuming she doesn't decide to go home, we've got eight hours left together—plenty of time to get this day back on track.

And when it's over . . . I'll finally tell Mom and Dad about Stanford. They're going to be upset. *Really* upset. But that's nothing compared to how they're going to react to the second part—the part I didn't tell April, and the *real* reason I've been putting this off for so long: I can't afford to go to college unless they help me pay for it. Because it turns out, financial aid covers my tuition, but it's not enough to pay for my housing or the mandatory Stanford health-care fee, not to mention whatever I need for books and dorm essentials. All in all, that's at least fifteen thousand dollars. And that's just for freshman year.

But I have to believe they're going to do it. Grandma thinks so, or at least she did, back when she made me promise to tell them the truth in exchange for covering the down payment. But then again, she thought I was going to say something months ago, not the day before I leave. Lucky for me, she believes we all have to make our own choices and live our own lives, so she's letting me do this my own way . . . but her patience is running out. I either tell them today, or she's going to tell them for me. Which would *not* be good.

So I'm going to tell them today. Or . . . maybe tonight. Definitely before midnight, no matter what. And then they'll know, and after some convincing, they'll agree to pay for the rest of my expenses. Everything will be all right, and tomorrow I'll get on a plane with Tom, and we'll start our new lives.

And if they *don't* say yes . . . then I'll just keep trying. Because staying in Los Angeles?

It's not an option.

CHAPTER 7

APRIL

hy couldn't she just have been honest?" I say into the phone, my voice so loud and full of anger that it scares away a flock of seagulls. "Or applied to some schools closer to home? This is total bullshit."

A lady with a baby strapped to her chest glares at me for my language, and I glare right back. "Oh, relax," I tell her. "He doesn't even *talk* yet."

On the other end of the phone, Nate sighs. "It's going to be weird working in the store without her."

"Forget the store," I say. "Do you know what it's going to be like living in my *house*? My parents fight all the time—"

"I know," he says. "I can hear them from next door sometimes."

The thought of Nate lying in bed, listening to my parents yell, makes me flush with embarrassment. "Exactly," I say, shaking it off. "And Jenn's the only one who can ever get them to stop. If she's gone, I don't know what'll happen."

"Do you think they might . . . divorce?" Nate asks.

"I don't know," I say. "I try not to think about it."

I look across the pier. Jenn is leaning against a railing, gazing out at the water. I know I should be happy for her. I *want* to be. But it makes me furious to see her there, looking like she doesn't have a care in the world, oblivious as usual to how I'm feeling. She doesn't understand that going to college doesn't just affect her—it affects me, too. Because without her, who's going to keep them from falling apart?

"They won't make it, Nate. I know they won't. And so does Jenn. That's why I don't understand how she can do this to them."

"Have you considered telling her that?"

"There's no point. It's not like my feelings about any of this matter to her. She's totally selfish."

"I guess . . ."

"What do you mean 'I guess'?"

Nate sighs. "You knew she was going to leave eventually, right? I know it sucks that you're not getting much warning—"

"I'm not getting *any* warning," I say, my voice loud again. "And neither are our parents!" I tug on one of my curls. "I still don't understand why she didn't just *tell us* she wanted to go to Stanford in the first place. It's not like anyone would have cared, and at least then we'd have some time to, I don't know, *plan*!"

I take a seat on a nearby bench and try to calm down.

"I can't believe I have to spend the rest of the day with her."

"So you're going to stay out, then?"

"I don't know," I say. "Jenn wants to finish the day."

"Huh. I'd think she'd want to spend her last day in LA saying goodbye to people. But maybe they already know she's leaving." He sighs again. "For someone so smart, your sister makes a lot of dumb choices."

"Tell me about it."

"Maybe you should keep going," Nate says. "It's your last chance to hang out with her before she moves."

I glance over at Jenn again. Her eyes are closed, and she's smiling up into the sun. It reminds me of all the times we lay on the roof of our apartment building as kids, pretending we were at the beach instead of avoiding Mom and Dad. Even though it scared me to hear them yelling at each other, those afternoons on the roof are some of my best memories of spending time with my sister. Jenn was so open, so honest back then. She'd let me ask questions about what was going on with our parents, and she'd talk to me about how *she* was feeling too. About how much she missed living near our grandma ever since she moved up north. The first time she told me she wanted to go away to college was on the roof too. And even though the idea of my big sister moving away terrified me, I was also excited for her. Because even then, I knew Jenn was going to want more than what our little rooftop could provide.

The anger in my chest loosens, but just a little. "Fine," I say. "I'll stay. But I'm not going to pretend what she did was okay."

"Good," Nate says. "Because it wasn't."

We say goodbye, and I head back toward where Jenn is waiting.

"Ready?" I ask when I reach her. "We're running behind again, so we should probably get going."

Jenn's face brightens. "So we're not going home?"

"No," I say. "But I'm still mad at you."

"Totally fair," she says.

I start to feel a little better—at least she's taking this seriously—but then she grins and my confidence disappears.

"What?" I demand. "Why are you smiling?"

"I get to hang out with you," she says. "Why wouldn't I be smiling?"

I want to believe her. It's the whole reason I put together this day—to cheer her up, and to spend time with her. But it's hard. She's yanked me around so much already, and it's not even ten a.m. But if I'm going to get through this day, I have to give her a little bit of a break, so I push down my suspicion and frustration and let her steer me back toward the parking garage.

When we reach the car, I pull out my key chain, but Jenn snatches it away from me. "I'm driving," she says, jingling the keys in the air.

"No way. Give them back."

She holds the keys above her head, like the two inches she's got on me is going to make a difference. I jump up, snatching them easily out of her hand.

"Ugh," she says. "I forgot you're sporty."

"I don't know how," I say. "I've been playing soccer for years."

She rolls her eyes. "It's not like there's jumping in soccer."

"Actually—never mind."

Jenn doesn't care about soccer—not since before Thomas—so there's really no reason to correct her. Just like there hasn't been a reason to tell her or my parents about my games in a long time, or how well I did during boot camp last month. But now that USC is interested in me, I can feel things changing. There's no way I'm telling her about it now, though. I've had enough of Jenn not giving a shit about me or my feelings for one day.

"Come on, let me drive," Jenn says. "I won't have a car freshman year, so this is one of my last chances."

"You don't even know where we're going!"

"Yeah, I do," she says. "We're going to Venice Beach. You showed me the list on your phone, remember?"

"Oh, right." The list didn't show what we're doing, but it *did* show where we're going.

"Fine," I say, tossing her the keys. "But don't take any weird detours. We're on a schedule."

"No weird detours," she says. "Got it."

I climb into the passenger side of the Prius and do my best not to wonder why it is that even when I'm the one making the plans, I still end up being along for the ride.

CHAPTER 8

JENN

When you say you're from LA, people immediately think of two things—traffic and celebrities. But there's so much more to it. Like the way the sun lights up the Santa Monica hills in the afternoon, or how the smell of the ocean gives way to the scent of candle stores and coffee shops on the promenade. They forget that LA is one of the most diverse cities in the country, and you can hear half a dozen different languages just walking down the street. Or how we have some of the best theater outside of New York City, and the best Mexican food outside of Mexico. They know a lot of people here are tan and laid-back, but what they miss is that they're all here for a reason—because they want something out of this city so badly that they're willing to put up with all that traffic to get it.

I don't know if it's seeing the sights of the last five years of my life flying by outside the window—the Urth Caffé, where Tom took me on our first date; the boutique my friend Katie's parents own — or if it's because I finally told someone in my family other than my grandma that I'm leaving LA, but as we fly down Lincoln Boulevard toward Venice Beach, a sudden rush of nostalgia for the city I grew up in overtakes me.

Unfortunately, the nostalgia is immediately followed by a strong bout of nervousness. It was one thing to tell Tom and my friends — they all understood why I needed to keep it a secret. But April said it herself: she's still angry. And angry people don't keep secrets. What if she texts Mom and Dad before I tell them tonight?

By the time we've circled the crowded beach neighborhood three or four times without finding a parking spot, I'm less focused on April ratting me out and more on keeping her from jumping out of the car. She hasn't said anything, but frustration is radiating off her like heat. She's never been patient, especially when it comes to parking.

I'm on the verge of paying for one of the exorbitant beach parking lots when I see a free spot. Actually, it's not *technically* a parking spot, but there's just enough room between another car and a large Dumpster to fit our compact Prius. Plus, the famous two-story-tall mural of shirtless Jim Morrison painted on the side of a building looms overhead, so I take that as a sign — Jim Morrison is one of Mom's favorite musicians. He wouldn't lead us astray. Plus, this is Venice. It's not like any of the beachy types that live here are going to call the cops.

April looks less sure. "Are you sure we can park here?" she asks.

"Totally."

I hop out of the car, but April's door doesn't open. I lean down and look at her through the window. "Are you coming?"

"Just a sec." She pulls down the sun visor and starts poking at her hair. Her curls were frizzy and dry like mine when we were younger, but sometime around middle school she developed dark brown Shirley Temple ringlets. I kept hoping mine were just running late, and that I'd wake up with picture-perfect curls like April's, but eventually I was forced to accept that I was either going to have to live with a curly mop on top of my head, or invest in a straightening wand.

"Your hair looks fine," I say. "Let's go!"

She finally gets out of the car, and I start down the block. But I've only taken a few steps when I realize April isn't following me. "What's wrong?"

"The ocean is that way," she says, pointing in the opposite direction.

"So?"

"So," she says, "that's where we're going."

I look down at my new leather flats and grimace. I should have looked at that list more closely. "Could we do something else instead?" I ask, careful to keep my voice friendly. "I'm not wearing the right shoes for the beach."

"We're not going to the beach. We're going to the boardwalk."

"Oh," I say. "Okay, then. Lead the way."

When we hit the boardwalk, April threads through the

crowd and keeps walking. I don't know how she does it—people just *move* for her, while I'm left struggling to get past a Rasta guy on a skateboard and an elderly couple with matching walkers. If it weren't for her curls bobbing along in the sea of people, I'd lose track of her completely. I finally catch up, and we stroll past the pizza shops and weed dispensaries, a thirtysomething with a snake wrapped around his neck, an old woman painting a henna tattoo onto a guy's shoulder, and a ten-year-old selling T-shirts with his own face on them. April might have been irritated with me a few minutes ago, but she's practically skipping now, and I have to admit, her excitement is infectious.

Then again, the snake handler staring at me probably is too.

"This is my favorite part," April says, pointing at the bright orange building that marks the site of Muscle Beach. She hurries over and leans on the metal fence that separates the boardwalk from the gated-off exercise area. A few of the bodybuilders on the other side are lifting weights, but most of them are strutting around, their oiled chests thrust out as they preen for the tourists watching from the sidelines.

I take a picture and send it to Tom. He sometimes jokes that the only way to get him in a gym is if there's a library inside it, so I add a few book emojis to go along with it.

This is the third text I've sent him this morning—once to say hello, and another time to tell him how the day was going—but he hasn't responded yet. My parents, however, have texted me not once, not twice, but three times *each*.

I quickly respond to their messages—**Where is the extra receipt paper? Will you please tell your mother she's wrong about how many people come into the store on Saturday afternoons? Why did you tell your father where the tax folder is? He needs to figure things out for himself!**—then drop my phone back into my purse.

"Sorry," I say. "Mom and Dad won't stop texting me."

April purses her lips. "That's nice."

"Not really," I mutter.

We stand in silence, watching the bodybuilders. Then April turns to me. "Have you figured out why I decided to bring you here yet?"

I bite my lip and try to think of some special memory April and I share here, but all my memories of Venice Beach are of me and my friends, or of me and Tom. "Not really."

April pulls out a photo from her purse and hands it to me. "Remember now?"

I study the photo. We're standing exactly where we're standing now, and we look only a few years younger, but beyond that nothing stands out. I don't want April to know that, though, so I smile and say, "Oh, yeah. Cool."

Her smile slips a little. "You don't remember it, do you?"

"No," I admit. "Sorry."

"It's from right before I started freshman year. I'd just made it onto the JV soccer team, and we were celebrating."

"Hmm . . ."

"You were really stressed about taking precalc," she prompts. "We practically had to tear you away from the textbook even though school hadn't started yet—"

"Oh!" I say. "I remember now. You scored a goal!"

"Yeah!" she says, her face lighting up. "Actually, it was an assist, but close enough."

I wait for April to tell me why she brought *me* here if this is really more about something that happened to *her*, but she doesn't say anything else. "Should we take a picture?" I ask. "We forgot to do one on the Ferris wheel."

"Yeah, sure." She takes out her phone and snaps a selfie of us.

"Nice," I say, when she shows it to me. But it's not. My mouth is pulled into what my friend Shruthi calls my "Diplomat Smile," which is to say, it's stiff and a little bit dead behind the eyes, but no one would be able to accuse me of not looking friendly. April, meanwhile, isn't even trying to smile. She just looks . . . bored.

April pulls out a pair of sunglasses and looks past Muscle Beach to the ocean in the distance. "Do you think you'll miss Venice Beach when you move away?"

"A little bit, but I can always visit when I come home for the holidays."

"I guess," she says. "But what about the ocean? If you move, you're going to really miss the ocean."

"Stanford is right *next* to the ocean."

"That's true . . . but it won't be the same."

Something in her voice gives me pause. Is she . . . sad? I try to read her face, but it's hard with the sunglasses. "Maybe that's a good thing," I say slowly. "Maybe change is exactly—"

A whistle blows, cutting me off. A Hispanic guy with huge arms and a teeny-tiny waist jumps the fence out of the gym area and strides into the middle of the boardwalk. "Who's ready for a show?" he calls.

People hesitate, not sure they want to interrupt their previously scheduled boardwalk activities. Mr. Muscle Beach holds up his arms and smiles. "Gather around, everyone," he says. "Don't be shy."

Suddenly, we're surrounded by tourists, all jostling for space to watch whatever is about to happen. "Let's go," I say, but April shakes her head. "I want to watch!"

People continue to crowd in, making a circle around him. I try to press my back up against the fence, but April grabs my hand and pulls me forward until we're right at the front.

Someone turns on a boom box that looks like it should be for sale in our antique store, and three more guys join him in the center. They start to perform—it's half dancing, half acrobatics—and the crowd pushes closer in, trapping April and me. A white guy wearing a backward baseball hat takes off his shirt, revealing a chest so cut it looks dangerous, and breaks through the line of dancers. They pretend to shove him, and he flies forward. For a second I think he's going to face-plant right there in front of us, but instead he kicks up into a handstand and begins to walk around the circle on his hands, his legs scissoring in the air as he dances upside down in time with the music. Everyone cheers.

Mr. Muscle Beach steps forward and lifts a cordless mic up to his mouth. "I need a volunteer!"

April's hand shoots into the air.

"Oh my god," I say. "Are you serious?"

"What?" she says. "It would be fun!"

I wave her off. "Don't be ridiculous, April."

Her expression turns stony. "You know what? You're right. It's *ridiculous* for me to go up there."

"Thank you."

"But it's a *great* idea for you to do it." And then, to my horror, she turns back to the front, cups her hands around her mouth, and yells, "We've got a volunteer over here!" She points at me. "Right here!"

"No!" I exclaim, but it's too late. The white guy in the hat is already grabbing my hand and pulling me forward.

"What's your name?" he asks.

"Jenn," I say, "but I don't—"

"Let's give a round of applause to Jenn!" he yells to the crowd.

Everyone claps, but I only have eyes for April. *I will kill you*, I mouth.

Worth it, she mouths back.

The guy in the hat takes the mic and calls out for more volunteers. While the crowd is distracted, Mr. Muscle Beach leans over so we're eye to eye. "You don't have to worry about a thing. Okay, chica?"

I blink stupidly at him, too nervous to speak.

"Hey, how old are you?" he asks. "Seventeen?"

"Eighteen," I answer.

"Same age as my sister, Mariana." He smiles. "Listen,

here's what's going to happen: I'm going to put you on my shoulder, and then I'm going to turn in a circle. Then I'm going to pick up another volunteer, and we're going to turn around again. When I'm done, I'm going to tell you both to fall backward."

"Backward?" I squeak.

"Yes. You're going to fall backward, and my homie Brian—the guy in the hat—is going to catch you. Okay?"

The words *hell no* are on the tip of my tongue, but if I say that he'll send me back to the crowd, and then everyone will know I was too scared to try and they'll all think I'm a wuss. April especially.

"Okay," I say reluctantly. "But if I hit the ground, I'm going to sue you."

He laughs. "You sound just like Mariana. Let's do this."

He turns back to the crowd and the music changes. It's all drums and bass, and I couldn't tell you what song it was if you paid me because the only thing I can think is, *Please don't let him drop me. Please don't let him drop me. Please—*

And then there are hands on my waist, and the next thing I know, I'm in the air. He doesn't lift me so much as *throw* me, but either way I suddenly find myself seated on his shoulder, at least six feet above the ground. I grip his other shoulder, but then I realize that I feel almost as secure up here as I would on a chair—his shoulder is just *that* wide. It also helps that he's got a death grip on my knees.

I look down, searching for April, but then Mr. Muscle Beach starts to turn in circles, just like he said he would. I start to grip his shoulder again, but then I realize . . . I'm not scared.

He eventually faces the front again, and a second later a woman around my mom's age pops up onto his other shoulder. She throws her arms into the air like I did, and the crowd goes bananas. But when Mr. Muscle Beach starts to turn around again, she yelps and covers her face.

"Don't worry," I call to her. "He won't drop you."

She uncovers her face. "I can't believe I'm doing this!"

"Me either!"

We eventually face front again, and I catch sight of April. She's staring up at me, her eyes wide—with shock or fear, I don't know—and suddenly I imagine myself from her perspective and start to laugh. If someone had told me when I woke up this morning that in a few short hours I'd be sitting on a stranger's shoulders in front of a cheering crowd, I would *never* have believed them.

"It looks like this one doesn't want to come down," Brian says into the mic.

For a second I'm not sure what he's talking about, but then I realize the woman who was next to me a moment ago has disappeared, and everyone is staring at me. I must have missed the signal to fall backward off his shoulder! I blush, but Brian is smiling. "I'm thinking it might be time to go surfing. What do you think, Marco?"

Mr. Muscle Beach—Marco—looks up at me. "You wanna do another trick?" he says, just loud enough for me to hear over the music.

I glance at April to see what she thinks, but she's too busy filming me to weigh in one way or the other. It's up to me. I could get down and no one would care. I've already done what they called me up here to do. But the surprising thing is . . . I don't *want* to get down. Maybe it's because I finally came clean to April, or maybe because tomorrow I'm starting fresh—new school, new city, new life—but for some reason the fact that this is an objectively terrible idea doesn't seem to bother me. After all, if I can survive telling a member of my family the truth, I can survive anything.

"I'm in," I tell Marco. "What do I have to do?"

"Nothing," he says. "Just relax and I'll take care of the rest."

I nod, and he leans forward just enough so that I slip off his shoulder. For a split second I think I've made a huge mistake—I'm going to hit the ground, and it'll be all my fault for agreeing to do this in the first place—but then he catches me behind the knees and back and cradles me in his ridiculously large arms, like a baby. The crowd cheers again.

"You ready?" Marco asks.

"I guess so."

"Good enough for me. Just don't squirm." He nods to Brian, who lifts the mic to his lips again.

"Let's count him down. Three—"

April covers her mouth, but I can tell she's smiling.

"Two—"

Marco bounces me in his arms, changing his grip on my back.

"One!"

Marco slowly begins to lift me. Not onto his shoulder like before, but directly over his head. It's slower, almost agonizingly slow, and I can feel the tremor in his arms as he pushes me into the air. I want to grab on to something but there's nothing to hold on to. All I can do is lie there on my back and pray he's as strong as he looks.

And then before I know it, I'm suspended high above his head, still flat on my back, though I keep glancing down at the audience below. At least fifty people are staring up at me, *ooh*ing and *aah*ing. And there at the front is April, cheering for me like I'm the one lifting Marco instead of the other way around. I give a tiny wave back—Marco might be strong, but I'm not tempting fate by moving around too much.

"Ready to come down?" Marco calls up to me.

"Yes!"

He lowers me back down to the ground and holds up his hand for a hive five. I give him a hug instead. "Thank you for not dropping me."

He laughs. "Thank you for not squirming."

I run back into the crowd, and April catches me in a hug. "You were great!" She lets go, and her face turns serious. "Are you pissed that I volunteered you?"

"Nah," I say. "I'm actually glad you did."

She looks surprised. "Really?"

"Yeah, really." I smile at her, and she smiles back.

"Ready for the next stop?" she asks.

"One thing first." I pull out my phone, turn on the

camera, and lean my head toward April. "Say 'cheese.'"

"Cheese!"

I snap the photo and drop my phone back into my purse. I might not remember the last time we came to Muscle Beach together, but I'll remember this forever.

CHAPTER 9

APRIL

I can't believe Jenn let that guy pick her up. It was like she'd been body snatched or something. I also can't believe she's not pissed at me for volunteering her. That's a small miracle in and of itself, and it almost makes me feel bad for doing it in the first place. *Almost*, but not quite. She's still got a long way to go before I stop being mad at her for springing Stanford on me.

We make our way off the boardwalk and back toward the car. I'm psyching myself up for telling her why I chose our next stop — Urth Caffé, where she and Thomas went on their first date, after which she looked like one of those heart-eyed emojis — when she stops walking.

"If we're going to do this pact thing," she says, "then I think we should do it together. You've got a plan, and I respect that, but can we squeeze in a few things I choose too?"

I fiddle with the car keys. I put a lot of time into making our itinerary, and I kind of want to show her what else I came up with. She had a good time at Muscle Beach, even though she clearly doesn't remember what she said to me that night. But that's okay—I do.

I'd just made the JV team an hour earlier, but instead of letting me go home to shower after the scrimmage, Mom and Dad had insisted we go to Venice Beach. Not to celebrate, of course, but because they'd heard about some tiny antique shop tucked away on a side street nearby and they wanted to check out the competition. Jenn didn't care about the antiques, though. She just cared about me making JV. So while Mom and Dad snooped, we snuck out to the boardwalk. *I can't believe how good you were out there*, she said as we leaned against the railings separating the boardwalk from Muscle Beach. *You should be so proud of yourself.*

Then she asked a stranger to take our picture.

It meant the world to hear her say she was proud of me. But I guess it didn't mean as much to her. If it did, she'd remember.

"Fine," I say, tossing her the keys. "We can alternate places. But I get to decide where we have lunch."

"Deal," she says. "But we don't need to drive. Our next stop is walking distance."

We set off, Jenn speed-walking like we're late to class, me hurrying after her. I'm just about to ask how much farther this mystery location is when she comes to an abrupt stop at the end of a long residential block. "Close your eyes," she says.

"Seriously?" I ask. "Why?

"Just trust me."

I close my eyes, and she takes my hand and pulls me around the corner. Jenn and I haven't held hands in years. It feels weird, but also familiar.

We come to a stop again, and she turns my body to the left. "Ta-da!" she says.

"No *way*." Stretching down the block where the street should be is a canal. A real-life canal, like the kind you'd find in Venice, *Italy*, not Venice *Beach*. Small canoes float in the water, each one docked in front of the owner's house. "Where did this come from?"

"It's always been here!" Jenn says. "Actually, this isn't the only one—there's a network of canals." She starts walking. "Come on—let's go stand on the bridge."

"There's a *bridge*?"

Sure enough, we walk another block, and halfway down the connecting canal is a bright white wooden bridge connecting the two walkways on either side. I walk to the middle and peer down. It's just high enough for a boat to pass under.

"Let's rent a canoe," I say. "Or a gondola. Whatever."

Jenn looks unsure. "I'm not sure we can. The canals are public, but I don't think they have rentals."

"There's gotta be a way." I turn around and look out over the other side of the bridge. "What's that?" I ask, pointing. "It's a boat, but it kind of looks like—"

"A pink swan!"

Jenn runs off the bridge and along the side of the canal. By the time I reach the swan boat, Jenn is bouncing on her toes and smiling so big I'm worried I'm going to have to sedate her. And it's no surprise—this boat looks like it was designed with Jenn in mind. My sister may be super serious most of the time, but she never really grew out of her ten-year-old obsession with pink. And this boat? It is *bright* pink. It looks like the kind of boat you'd ride in It's a Small World at Disneyland.

"I wish we could borrow it," Jenn says.

"Hmm." I look up and down the canal, then step into the boat and crouch down.

"April!" Jenn exclaims. "What are you doing?"

"Looking for the oars, obviously."

Jenn glances over her shoulder, then takes a step closer to the boat. "We are not going to borrow this boat without asking," she whispers. "We could be arrested!"

I reach under the seat, and pull out two bright pink oars. Figures. "We'll leave a note," I say. "Come on!"

She crosses her arms. "No way."

"Don't be a—"

The front door to the house directly behind Jenn opens and an old man appears in the doorway. "What are you two doing?" he demands.

"Nothing," I say, jumping out of the boat.

"Doesn't look like nothing." He steps forward, letting the door close behind him. "That boat doesn't belong to you," he says. "You shouldn't be in there."

"We were just—" I start, but Jenn steps in front of me.

"We're so sorry, sir," she says, her voice sweet as honey.

"We were just so *amazed* by the canals, and then we saw your adorable boat, and I thought we could take a quick picture without bothering anyone. My sister didn't want to do it because, like you said, it's not our boat, but I insisted. You see, our grandmother just *loves* swans, so I thought—"

"Oh, all right, all right," the man says, holding up his hands. "Take your picture."

I climb back into the boat, and Jenn clambers in after me. I take my cell phone out of my purse, and we snap a selfie.

"That's not going to be a very good picture," the man observes. "Your grandma won't even be able to tell it's a swan from that angle."

"Oh," Jenn says, glancing at me. "Right . . ."

"Give it here," he says, striding down his walkway toward us. "I'll take the photo."

I hand my phone over. I half expect him to fumble with it and complain about "newfangled smartphones," but instead he takes a step back, lifts the phone, and snaps a picture. "Let me get another angle," he says, taking a step to his left. "This time, look like you actually have a grandma who is waiting on this photo, and not just a big sister who has a future in politics."

Jenn tenses next to me, but I burst out laughing. The old man smiles and takes another picture. "That's a good one."

He hands the phone back to me. He's right—it's a great picture. Way better than the selfies we've been taking.

Jenn starts to climb out, but he stops her. "You girls want

to take Alice here out for a bit? I almost never use her anymore; it'd be nice to see her out on the water."

"Your boat's name is Alice?" I ask.

He nods. "After my wife. She died last summer."

"I'm so sorry," Jenn says, but he waves her off. "Have fun, and get her back by dark."

"Oh, we don't need that long," I say as Jenn settles into a seat and picks up the pink oars. "Just twenty minutes."

"Suit yourself," he says, pulling a key out of his pocket. He unlocks the boat's mooring from the dock. "Just make sure you lock her back up when you're finished."

"Thank you," Jenn and I both say.

"You're welcome." Then he puts his shoe on the swan's folded wooden wing and pushes us away from the side of the canal.

Jenn fumbles the oars into the water and starts to row. I peer over the edge. "It's not very deep. Or clean. Where does the water come from?"

"The canals lead to the marina, which connects to the ocean."

"So this is salt water?" I ask as a duck floats by in the water beside us. "That explains why it still kinda smells like the beach."

We continue to paddle down the canal, past landscaped front gardens full of lavender and rosemary, and a house shaped like a small castle. I lean against the back of the swan's neck and tilt my face up to the sun. It's midmorning, but the day is starting to heat up. I look at the houses floating by, and even though I'm still kind of mad at my sister for lying to me, I have to admit that hanging out with her is really nice. She seems way less tense than usual—like telling me the truth made her lighter somehow. I just wish she'd done it sooner.

Jenn's phone buzzes.

"Thomas?" I ask.

"No," she replies. "Just Mom, checking in. You know how she is."

"Not really," I say. "Mom doesn't text me."

Jenn's eyebrows shoot up. "She doesn't?"

"Nope. Unless she can't find *you*. Then I hear from her."

She goes quiet, and I think maybe it's finally sinking in for her that Mom and Dad don't pay attention to me. That she is their priority, and I am an afterthought. At best.

But then she sighs and starts rowing again. "Must be nice," she says.

I stare at her. *Must be nice?* To be ignored and forgotten? No, I want to insist. *It's not nice. I'm a stranger in my own home. I'm an inconvenience. I'm not good enough to notice, and never will be. It's not nice at all.* But even if I say these things, Jenn won't understand. She can't, not really. Mom and Dad worship the ground she walks on. They have for years, ever since it became clear she was destined for academic greatness like the two of them, and I . . . wasn't.

For a while, it seemed like that might be okay. Up until ninth grade, they were still coming to my soccer games, still cheering me on from the sidelines. Sure, we spent every night talking over dinner about which honors classes Jenn was testing into, and every morning wishing her good luck on yet another test she was sure to ace, but at least they were showing up to games once a week. But then Mom and Dad opened the store, and they stopped coming to games. I thought they'd at least ask how I was playing, but instead it was like they forgot I played soccer entirely. They forgot about *me* entirely. But Jenn? They always kept her in their sights, no matter what. And Jenn ate it up.

Jenn looks up at me. "You should start thinking about which shifts you're going to pick up."

"What do you mean?"

"At the store. Now that I'm leaving, I mean." She leans forward, pushing the top of the oars all the way to my knees, then pulls back, taking them with her. We surge forward in the water. "Obviously, you can't go until after your classes are over during the week, but have you thought about whether you want to work in the morning or afternoons on the weekend?"

"Uh, no. Because I'm not doing any of that."

She frowns. "What do you mean?"

"Jenn, I'm not working in the store. That's your thing, not mine."

"No, that's our *family's* thing," she says. "Mom and Dad are going to need you to start helping out. Especially on Saturdays. That's the busiest day."

"I can't. I have practice on Saturday."

"Practice for what?" she asks.

I immediately want to throttle her. "Soccer! Why is everyone always forgetting I play *freaking* soccer?"

Jenn's eyes go wide, and I realize I just yelled at her in the middle of this quiet canal. I take a deep breath and try to regain my cool. "Look, I'm on varsity this year, okay? Which means we practice every day after school from four till six, and we have tournaments in the evenings and on weekends."

"Can't you just, I don't know, skip some of that? Or move it around?"

"Are you serious?" When she doesn't say anything, I say, "No, I can't skip it, and I can't just *move it around*. If I miss that stuff, I'll get kicked off the team."

Jenn keeps rowing. "It's just a hobby. It's not like soccer actually matters for your future."

Her words hit me like a blow. She's talking about soccer, but dismissing it like that—like it's not worth discussing, like this thing I love is worthless—it cuts all the way down to my bones. Because she's *not* just dismissing soccer. She's dismissing *me*.

Not only does Jenn not remember what she said to me at Muscle Beach, she never meant it in the first place. If it's not academics, it doesn't matter to her. Or to my parents, for that matter. That's why I didn't bother telling them when I made varsity—because who cares about sports when there are calculus textbooks to read and shitty antiques to polish? Never mind that a soccer scholarship could get me into college despite my grades only being middle-of-the-road. Never mind that it makes me *happy*.

This is the time to tell her about the USC rep. Right here, right now. She'd have to take it seriously then. But I don't want anyone to know about it, not when there's no guarantee it will work out. The only thing worse than listening to her talk about my dreams like they're a joke would be watching her face if it turns out she's actually right.

"Soccer is part of who I am," I say at last, my voice shaking with barely controlled rage. "It's *not* just a hobby."

"I know it's fun," Jenn says slowly, like I'm a child. "And I'm not saying you should give it up entirely. I just think it's time for you to look past what's fun and focus more on what's important. Like family. And college."

"That's pretty funny, coming from someone who *lied* to her family for a year about exactly that."

Jen glares at me. "I thought we were past that."

I cross my arms. "You thought wrong."

We continue to float down the canal, but the entire mood has changed. I'm trapped in this stupid boat. Not just with my sister, but with the awful realization that Jenn's right. There's no way Mom and Dad won't make me work at the store once they find out she's leaving. It won't matter that I have other things going on or that I hate being cooped up with all that old crap. With Jenn gone, I'll have no choice.

I'll lose the only part of me that matters.

"I know it's disappointing," Jenn says, reaching for the oars once more, "but sometimes you have to make sacrifices. That's part of growing up."

I dig my fingernails into my palms. It's one thing to not give a shit about what happens to me, but it's another to act like *I'm* the one who's hurting this family. She's the one who's abandoning us. She's the one who doesn't care what it'll be like for me, being on my own with Mom and Dad. I thought things were bad already, but at least Jenn's presence keeps them from tearing each other's heads off. Without Jenn here to stop them . . . who knows what'll happen?

She can't do this. I won't let her.

The truth hits me so hard and fast that I almost gasp: no matter what it takes, my sister has to stay in LA. Yes, she'll be sad for a while, but there are other great schools besides Stanford. Like UCLA or USC, both of which are within driving distance. Or, if she's really set on Stanford, she could defer her enrollment and then go a year from now, once we have everything figured out. Once Mom and Dad are more stable, or they've hired someone to help out at the store. By then I'll have already met the USC rep, and hopefully secured a soccer scholarship. But until then? She can't go.

I won't let her.

My phone buzzes in my bag, and I grab it like a lifeline. I'd rather talk to a telemarketer than Jenn right now. Luckily, it's far better than a spam banking call. It's a text message from Eric, asking what I'm doing. *Thank goodness.* I didn't ruin things between us by texting about my fight with Jenn after all.

I'm floating in a pink boat on the canals of Venice, I answer.

His answer comes right away. **Pics or it didn't happen.**

I'm not exactly in the mood to take a selfie, but I don't want to disappoint him, so I shake my hair out and then snap a photo. I check the picture, and immediately notice I've got a weird shadow on my face and my cheeks look flushed because of the reflection of the sunlight off the pink bird. I take another and check the picture again—much better.

When I'm finished sending it to him, I look up to see Jenn shaking her head. "I don't know why you bother talking to him."

"Who?" I ask.

"Eric Randall. That's who that was, right? He's a jerk."

I shove my phone into my purse. Is there anything Jenn *won't* criticize me about today? "You don't know what you're talking about. You've only spoken to him once, and it was in the middle of the night."

Jenn pulls the oars out of the water and lets us float. "I don't need to talk to him for hours to know he's a jerk." She smirks. "I just need to look at him."

"That's ridiculous," I say. "And super judgmental."

"You're calling *me* judgmental? April, you are one of the judgiest people I have ever met. You and Nate both are." She smirks. "That's why you're perfect for each other."

"Don't be stupid."

"I'm not stupid. I'm very smart. Which is why you should listen to me when I tell you that Eric Randall is a jerk and you're better off without him." She dips the oars back into the water and mutters, "If you even *have him* in the first place."

"Excuse me?"

"I'm just saying, I know you've been sneaking him into your room—"

"Which I'm sure you find totally inappropriate and immature, right?"

"I don't find it immature, but I *do* think it's ill-advised. Are you guys even dating?"

"No," I snap. "Not yet. But that doesn't mean we can't hook up. What are you, a nun?"

"No! I just don't want you to get involved in something you can't handle."

I yank one of the oars away from her. I'll be less tempted to smack her if my hands are busy. "I can handle myself just fine. I don't need you telling me what to do. Or your holier-than-thou bullshit advice on relationships."

"Maybe you *do*, since I'm the one with a boyfriend and you're the one sending selfies to a guy who's probably texting with half a dozen other girls."

My breath hitches. "That's—that's not true."

"I mean, I don't know for sure," Jenn says, backpedaling. "But he's got a reputation for going out with a lot of girls at once and not telling them about it. You know that, right?"

I squeeze the handle of the oar. "Those are just rumors. He likes me and I like him."

"But does he *really* like you?" Jenn asks quietly. "Or does he just like having sex with you?"

My mouth drops open, and the oar slips into the water and falls off the boat. "Shit!"

Jenn and I both lunge to grab it. Her shoulder collides with mine, throwing me off balance. I scream and grab at the side of the boat. But it's too late—I tumble into the water.

The canal is warm and murky, and my mouth floods with brackish water. I spit it out as I struggle to my feet. "What the hell!" I yell at Jenn.

"I'm sorry!" she says. "I didn't mean to!"

I wade over to the side of the boat, and Jenn immediately scoots away from the edge, her face fearful.

"Oh, please," I say. "I'm not going to pull you in."

She nods, but I can tell she doesn't really believe me, which makes me even more furious. If one of us should be suspicious of the other, it's *me*.

"Give me my purse," I demand, and she hands it to me. Then I turn and start to wade the other way, back toward the bank of the canal. Nasty water drips down my curls into my face. I wipe it away, but it doesn't do any good. I'm completely soaked.

I hoist myself up onto the bank and stand, water pouring off of me. "I want to go home. I'll meet you back at the car."

"Okay, but wait for me," Jenn says, struggling to turn the boat around with just one oar. "I just have to . . ."

But I don't listen to the rest of what she says. She's hurt me enough for one day.

CHAPTER 10

JENN

I screwed up. I screwed up *bad*.

I didn't mean to hurt April's feelings, and I *definitely* didn't mean to knock her into the canal. I just wanted to help. She thinks I'm some kind of prude, but I don't care if she has sex. That's up to her. But I *do* care if she's having sex with someone who doesn't give a shit about her. I may have only spoken to Eric Randall once, but I already knew him by reputation, and one thing is *very* clear: He doesn't care about anyone but himself. He didn't care about Donna from our AP Bio lab, or Kristen from Homecoming, or Keisha from camp when we were fourteen. He's a player, pure and simple, and my little sister deserves better than that. Everyone does.

But that doesn't mean what I said was okay. Not even a little bit. So as soon as I get back to the car, I'm going to apologize. But first I need to get this stupid bird back to its owner.

I retrieve the lost paddle, which has luckily resurfaced,

then turn myself back the way we came. But after a few minutes of paddling, I realize hurrying back to the car might be the wrong move. It might be a good idea to give April some time to cool—and dry—off.

Instead, I rest the oars and text Tom for the fourth time this morning. I haven't heard from him, but I'm trying not to worry. Sometimes he likes to take a walk in the morning to clear his head before he starts his day. Maybe he lost his phone along the way. Or maybe he forgot to charge it, and now it's sitting forgotten by his bed, the screen lit up by my texts.

But a voice in the back of my head has been whispering that something might be wrong, and now that I'm sitting alone in this boat, I can't help but listen to it.

I pick up my phone and dial. It rings once, and I settle in to wait, but instead the call abruptly goes to voicemail in the middle of the second ring.

Hello, you have reached Thomas Albert. I can't come to the phone right now—

I hang up and try again, just in case the connection is bad, and the same thing happens. Except this time it rings twice. *Hello, you have reached—*

A sinking feeling comes over me, and I drop my phone on the seat next to me. Everyone knows that when a phone only rings once or twice before abruptly going to voicemail it means the other person is screening their calls. My friend Katie calls it "hitting the fuck-you button." But there must be another explanation. Bad service? Maybe it's not a good time to talk? I look at my phone, resting quietly beside me, and wait for a text message to arrive saying he'll call me back. But the seconds turn to minutes, and as I continue to row the boat back to the dock, a new possibility occurs to me.

Is Tom mad at me?

I pick up the oar and try to channel my worries into rowing. But I can't help going over the problem in my head. Why would he be mad? We disagreed last night, but it was hardly worth giving me the silent treatment over. *But he didn't say "I love you" after you hung up last night*, that voice whispers again. *Maybe you did something and you just don't know it.*

I reach the dock, haul myself out of the boat, and lock up the bird. There's no sign of the owner, so I leave the key inside the boat then hurry back toward Venice Beach. I'm going to drop April off, then immediately go to Tom's house. I might not even drop her off first. Maybe she can—

My phone rings. I stop walking and scramble to answer it. "Tom?"

"Um, no," Katie says. "Not Tom."

"Oh," I say. "Hi."

"Don't sound so excited," she says.

"Sorry. I've just been trying to reach Tom all morning, and he's not answering."

"Weird," Katie says. "I'm sure he's fine, though. Probably just busy packing or whatever. Which brings me to why I'm calling you. Actually—hold on. Shruthi wants me to put you on speaker."

There's a shuffling noise, and then Shruthi's voice comes

through, clear and determined. "Katie and I have decided that you need a proper send-off before you leave for Stanford."

"We just had a party last week!" I say. "I don't need another one."

"Not a party," Katie says. "Lunch. Just the three of us. What do you think?"

I bite my lip. Technically I agreed to have lunch with April, but it's only eleven, and she *did* just say she wants to go home. But then I think about all the packing I still have to do, not to mention the fact that I still haven't told my parents I'm leaving. "I don't know, you guys, I have a lot to do today. . . ."

"I told you she'd say no," Katie mutters.

"Jenn, please consider the facts," Shruthi says. "You are leaving tomorrow, and will be gone for at least six months. We haven't seen you since last week. Lunch is only going to take an hour, plus the ten minutes it will take to drive to and from your house to the restaurant, and you have to eat anyway—"

"Fine, fine," I say. "The defense rests! Stop lawyering me."

"Oh my gosh," Katie says, "you should see how happy Shruthi looks right now."

"Shut up," Shruthi says, laughing. She's wanted to be a lawyer for as long as I've known her, and spends every free moment watching *Law & Order* reruns. I told her that show isn't even real, but she insists it's still based on case law. I also think she has a crush on the young cop with the good hair, but she won't admit it.

"When should we meet?" I ask. "And where?"

"It has to be a little bit late," Shruthi says. "I promised I'd take my sister to the mall at one o'clock to buy party favors."

"What is she getting?" Katie asks. "Candy?"

"I wish," Shruthi says. "She wants to hand out neon yellow fanny packs. I tried telling her they're lame, but she said the nineties are back and I need to get with the program."

"Hold up," I say. "Isn't your sister turning, like, seven?"

"Uh-huh. But she reads *Teen Vogue* when my mom isn't looking."

"Focus!" Katie says. "How about In-N-Out at two? The one on Washington?"

"Perfect," I say. "See you guys then."

We hang up, and I immediately check to see if Tom texted me while I was on the phone.

He didn't, but Grandma did.

Did you tell them yet, sweetheart? I don't want to be a pain, but please don't forget our agreement.

I grip the phone so hard I almost drop it. **Not yet, but I will!** ☺

Okay. Let me know when it's done, please.

"Will do," I mutter. Then I slip my phone into my bag and head back toward the beach.

CHAPTER 11

APRIL

I squish my way toward the car, my waterlogged shoes leaving wet footprints on the sidewalk. I can't believe Jenn expects me to give up soccer to work in the store even though she knows I hate it there. And all that bullshit about sacrificing for the family? Jenn's never sacrificed a thing in her life. Mom and Dad would sooner lie down in the middle of the road than ask her to give up something that's important to her.

She also has no right to say Eric is only interested in me for sex. It's true that we don't talk a ton in person, but we text all the time. He says he misses me sometimes, and I hear from him almost every day. He also remembered my birthday last month without me having to tell him it was coming up, *and* he's been hinting hard lately that he has something to tell me. It's gotta be that he wants to be my boyfriend. What else could it be?

The mural of Jim Morrison's skinny chest comes into

view up ahead, and my pace quickens. I want to go home, change my clothes, and forget today ever happened. Except when I get closer, I realize that's not going to happen. Not any time soon, anyway. Because the car?

It's gone.

I spin in a slow circle, as if maybe the car just *moved* a few spots away. A group of tourists pass, eyeing me like I'm some kind of sideshow. I know what they must be thinking—*Look at that soaking-wet idiot who lost her car. That would never happen to me.* I plop down on the curb. What am I going to do? If Jenn were here—

No. I don't need Jenn. I can handle this by myself. I unlock my phone. Normally, I would call Nate and ask him for help, but I have something better in mind.

"Hi," I say when Eric picks up. "Do me a *huge* favor?"

"We could have just called a Lyft, you know," Jenn says for the second time. "Or Tom. *He* would be here by now."

I grit my teeth and continue to play games on my phone. "Eric said he'd be here in twenty minutes. It's only been twenty-five. Just relax."

"Don't tell me to—"

A car honks. "Aww," a voice calls, "I was hoping I'd get here before you dried off."

I smile and hop up. Eric is leaning out the window of his dad's bright blue Audi. His blond hair looks almost white in the sun. I run over to the car. When I reach him, he whispers, "Can I kiss you in front of your sister?"

I glance back at Jenn. She looks skeptical, like she's not sure Eric is *actually* going to help us even though he drove all this way. I turn back to him and nod.

He hooks his finger into the belt loop of my jeans and pulls me toward him. I bend over and he kisses me. It's fast but deep, like he wants to have as much of me as he can while he can, and I shiver despite the sun on my back. When we part, he looks past me to Jenn. "Hey, Jennifer," he calls. "Are you coming or should I send someone else to pick you up?"

I swat at him. "Be nice."

He grins. "Nope."

Jenn comes over to the car. "Thank you for picking us up," she says in her best polite-despite-your-rudeness voice. "Please take us to the impound lot on Lincoln and Ocean Park Boulevards. That's where the car is."

He makes a mock-serious face and salutes her, and I'm reminded of Nate doing the same yesterday in the kitchen. Except when he did it, it didn't feel sarcastic so much as play-ful. If he was here, he'd probably be extra nice to Jenn even though she's the one who chose the dumb not-a-parking-spot that got the car towed in the first place. He insists she's not that bad once you get to know her, like working with her at the antique store has given him insight into my sister that I've somehow just missed during the sixteen years I've lived with her. It's sweet that he can see the best in everybody, though. It's one of my favorite things about him.

Jenn and I climb in, and Eric starts the car. "Ready for

the best part?" He pushes a button on the dash, and the roof starts to move.

"I didn't know this was a convertible!"

"Of course it is," Jenn mumbles from the back. I turn around in my seat to face her. "This is Eric's dad's car," I say meaningfully. "Isn't it *nice* that he let Eric *borrow* it, especially at the last minute?"

She purses her lips. "Yes. Very nice."

Satisfied, I turn back around. Eric reaches over and laces his fingers through mine and starts to drive. But the moment he takes a turn, Jenn leans forward.

"This isn't the way to Lincoln Boulevard," she says.

"We're taking the freeway to get there," Eric explains. "There was an accident, so the streets are practically a parking lot. Plus, sitting in traffic in a convertible is lame. You'll just get hot baking in the sun. Trust me."

Jenn sits back. "Fine, but please don't speed. The last thing I need is to have this thing flip and kill us all."

I cringe, but Eric laughs. "You're the boss."

Eric navigates the car onto the freeway, and soon we're heading east. We turn on the radio and KROQ blasts out of the speakers. Eric lets out a whoop that's immediately swept away by the wind, then grabs my hand and kisses it, sending a rush of warmth through me. This is what I like about Eric. When I'm with him, I don't have to think about what's going on with my family, or school, or anything else. I can just get swept up in his world and how good it feels to be wanted.

"Put your hands up!" he calls over the radio. I disentangle

my fingers from his and reach up into the wind. Someday I want to have a convertible, and since it never rains in LA, I won't ever have to put the top up. I'll drive around like this all the time, carefree and alive like Eric. And maybe he'll even be there by my side, just like he is now.

Something touches my stomach, and I jerk my arms back down. Eric's warm hand is on my side, just underneath my shirt. I push him away. "Not in front of my sister."

He glances back at her in the rearview mirror. "She's texting."

"Still."

He puts his hand back on the wheel. "Suit yourself."

My phone rings, and Nate's name lights up the screen. "Hey," I answer, "what's up?"

"Where are you? It's super loud."

I glance at Eric. I'm not sure why, but I don't want to tell Nate I called Eric to pick us up instead of him. "In the car with Jenn. Where are you?"

"I'm at the store."

"Oh, right. How's it going?"

"Eh, fine. Better than being at home."

"Since when?"

The line goes quiet. I adjust the phone to my other ear and ask, "Are you still there?"

"Yeah," Nate says. "My mom is just on my case. It's no big deal."

I glance at Eric, then angle myself away. "Hey," I say quietly, "are you okay? If you need to talk, I could—"

"I'm fine," Nate says immediately. "How's it going with Jenn?"

"Not great," I say, keeping my voice low. "She pushed me into a canal and then got our car towed because she parked illegally near the beach."

"Holy crap," he says. "Are you okay?"

I look in the rearview mirror at Jenn. She's pressed as close to the door as possible with her arms crossed. Only Jenn could make a ride in a convertible seem like a chore. "I'm fine," I say. "Just . . . frustrated."

"I don't blame you," Nate says.

Jenn looks up and catches my eye in the mirror. "What?" she asks. "Why are you looking at me like that?"

"Shit," Nate says. "A customer just walked in. He probably only wants to use the bathroom, but I should go."

"Okay," I say. "Let me know if you change your mind and want to talk, okay?"

Nate sighs. "Yeah. I will."

We hang up just as Eric is exiting the freeway. "Who was that?" he asks over the radio.

I reach over to take his hand again. His fingers are warm, and they immediately interlace with mine. "Nate."

He shakes his head. "He's weird. I don't trust a guy with that many female friends. Like, what are you trying to prove, you know?"

"He's not trying to *prove* anything," I say. "We're his friends."

"Seems like he's just riding the friend zone to victory, if you ask me."

Jenn leans forward, so her head is between the seats, and turns off the radio. "The friend zone is a ridiculous myth propagated by the patriarchy to make *boys* feel like *women* owe them something," she says. "But women don't owe anyone anything, least of all sex. Either you're a friend or you're not."

"No need to be so uptight," Eric says. "Relax."

I look at him sharply. "Don't tell her to relax."

Eric rolls his eyes and pulls his hand away from me. "Whatever."

We drive in uncomfortable silence for a few minutes. I cross my arms, and lean my head back against the headrest. I'm not sure what bugs me more, that Eric is being a jerk, or that my sister called him out on it, but I think it actually might be the first one. Just because Eric and I are probably going to start officially dating doesn't mean he's allowed to be rude to her.

The sign for the impound comes into view ahead. "That's the lot," I say, pointing.

"Thank god," Eric mutters.

Jenn climbs out as soon as the car stops moving and she goes into the office. I turn in my seat to face Eric. The conversation got tense there for a minute, but I want to smooth things over. If we're going to date for real, we'll have to get through an argument now and then. "Thank you for the ride."

He looks out the front windshield at my sister. "Are you hanging out with her all day?"

"I'm not sure," I admit. "I'm kind of pissed at her right now, but we had this whole plan to spend the day together—"

He snorts. "Why?"

I fiddle with my seat belt as I try to decide how to answer him. Part of me wants to say, *Why* wouldn't *I* spend the day *with her? She's my sister.* But a little over twenty-four hours ago I was basically asking Nate the same question Eric is asking me now, and it's not like I'm feeling particularly happy with her at the moment anyway. I also *really* don't want to get into another argument with him. It's one thing when it happens with my sister or Nate—I know they'll forgive me if I say something stupid or a little too mean. But something about disagreeing with Eric makes me feel nervous, like I might say the wrong thing and ruin everything. So I change the subject instead.

"What are you doing tonight?" I ask. "Do you want to hang out?"

He puts the car into reverse. "I would, but I've got some things to do at home with my dad."

"Oh," I say, disappointed. "Okay." I unbuckle my seat belt but don't get out. "Then . . . I'll see you tomorrow?"

"Let's play it by ear." He leans toward me and gives me a quick kiss on the cheek. "Bye."

I climb out of the car, my heart in my throat, but before I have a chance to ask him if he's upset with me, he's already backing out onto the street. When I turn to go inside, I find Jenn standing in the doorway. "You okay?" she asks.

The truth—that I'm worried he's mad at me, that I'm

worried I might be mad at him, that maybe everything is ruined now—swirls inside me. But I can't tell Jenn any of that. She won't understand. Her relationship with Tom is airtight. And besides, she's already made it pretty clear she doesn't like Eric. The last thing I want to do is admit maybe . . . just *maybe* . . . he's not as great as I thought.

"I'm fine," I say, plastering on a fake smile. Besides, it's not like she really cares.

CHAPTER 12

JENN

I take a seat while we wait for the man behind the counter to prepare our paperwork. April lingers outside for a few minutes, pacing in the sun, then eventually comes in and sits as far from me as possible. Which isn't very far, considering how small the office is, but I get the message all the same: She doesn't want to talk to me.

I get that it sucks to have your sister arguing with your boyfriend. But that's the thing—Eric *isn't* her boyfriend. He's just a jerk who tricks girls into thinking he likes them and then ditches them as soon as he gets what he wants. And as much as I love my sister, I'm pretty sure she doesn't have enough experience to recognize a player when she sees one. If she did, she wouldn't be with someone like Eric. She'd be with someone who cares about people and treats them with respect, like Tom.

Not that Tom is being a particularly great boyfriend today either. He still hasn't returned any of my calls or texts, and it's too late in the day for me to keep kidding myself that he just hasn't had a chance to look at his phone. But I'm going to give him the benefit of the doubt. Not just because he deserves it, but because he'd do the same for me. He already has, really. I know he's frustrated with me for not talking to my parents about Stanford yet. That might even be why he's not answering my calls—because he wants me to talk to *them*, not him. But he's still been waiting patiently for me to tell them for months, ever since the acceptance letter came in the mail in the first place.

Ever since I handed it to them . . . and they told me I couldn't go.

I try not to let myself think about it, because it makes me so angry I can barely sit still. But sitting in this dingy room with Grandma's threat looming over me, I can't help but remember.

I was so excited when my admission packet arrived in the mail. The package was warm from sitting in the mailbox all day, first while I was at school, and later while I was working at the store. I didn't bother grabbing the letter opener out of Mom's office. Instead, I plopped down on the floor just inside the front door and tore open the envelope. *Congratulations! It is with great pleasure that I offer you admission to Stanford University.*

I screamed so loud that it set off a car alarm outside. I had done it. After years of hard work, of falling asleep to dreams of Stanford's beautiful campus and the freedom it would provide me, I had gotten in. I was going to college. And not just any college. My dream school.

Then my parents came home. We were supposed to be going to Uncle Chris's birthday party that night—the perfect opportunity to tell my entire family my amazing news. But the moment Mom and Dad walked through the door, their faces flushed and fists clenched, I knew it wasn't going to happen. Then April came downstairs, probably thinking we were about to leave, and I thought, *Maybe this time she can help me. I'll show her the acceptance letter and she'll* have *to help.* But then Mom and Dad's argument started up again, and April immediately pushed past them through the front door and headed to Nate's house. Leaving me, as usual, to deal with the fallout.

But for once I didn't. Getting away from Mom and Dad was the whole point of moving away, and as far as I was concerned, my new life was starting right then and there. So instead of calming them down, I handed Mom my acceptance letter and went to bed. Or I tried to. Turns out it's hard to fall asleep when words like "divorce" and "I'm leaving" are being shouted one floor below you. It took everything I had to stay in bed and let them figure things out on their own, but I did it. I stayed out of it and eventually fell asleep.

It wasn't until the next morning, when I came down to find them standing side by side in the kitchen, that I realized what a huge mistake I'd made.

We can't possibly run the store without you, Mom said.

It'd close within weeks, Dad agreed. *There's no way we could stay afloat.*

I begged them to reconsider. I reminded them of how

hard I had worked, of all the hours I'd put in, not only at the store but with my long list of extracurriculars—clubs and volunteer groups and after-school peer tutoring. But it was as useless. For once, they were united. I was staying in LA so that I could continue to work at the store. It was my duty as a member of the family. No amount of arguing would make a difference, and by the time Dad put his hand on my shoulder and said, "What would we do without you?" it was as if the idea to stay in LA and go to community college had been mine all along.

I glance over at April. She's sitting with her body angled away from me so I can't see her face, but I can tell from the hunch of her shoulders that she's still angry. I want to feel bad—for what I said about Eric, and for lying to her—but I can't. Everything I've done has been for her own good. I'm protecting her from Eric just like I protected her from the truth about Mom and Dad: that they might love us, but at the end of the day, they'll put themselves first every time.

And maybe I'm protecting myself a little bit too. Because even as I sit here, remembering my parents' faces as they told me they couldn't keep the store open without me, a part of me wonders if that's really why they needed me to stay. If it was the store they were really worried about . . . or themselves.

CHAPTER 13

APRIL

Parking under Jim Morrison turns out to be a two-hundred-dollar mistake. I use a payment app to send Jenn my half, even though I *told* her that wasn't a stupid parking spot, then we follow the impound employee out to the car. He points at the Prius, grunts, then leaves.

"So . . . home?" Jenn asks when we're alone.

I look down at myself. My jeans are almost dry, but I can smell the stale canal water on me. I can't believe I let Eric see me like this. Sweat after soccer is one thing, but there's nothing remotely sexy about smelly canal water. "Yeah. If I don't get out of these clothes I'm going to puke."

We get into the car, and I immediately turn up the radio so I don't have to talk to my sister. But as we pull out of the driveway and turn toward home, I remember that I'm supposed to convince her to stay in LA, and that's not going to happen if we aren't speaking.

"Jenn, I want to talk to you about something," I say as I turn off the radio.

"Yeah?"

"It's about you leaving." I stare out the window, not letting myself look at her. If I do, I might lose my nerve. "I've been thinking about it all morning, and I'm worried about what it'll be like when you're gone."

There's silence for a moment, then Jenn says, "I am too."

"Really?"

She nods. "I meant to tell you this earlier, but then the car got towed, and we had to get a ride, and I guess I got distracted." She takes a deep breath and tightens her hands on the steering wheel. "I'm sorry about what I said in the boat. I'm just concerned, you know? About what's going to happen to you if I'm not here to help."

I sit back in my seat, my whole body suddenly weak with relief. I knew Jenn would come around. She's always been the one to hold our family together. A person doesn't just stop doing that overnight. And everything she said about me quitting soccer to take over her shifts—no one is *that* selfish.

"I don't want to do this without you," I say. "It would just be a lot to handle on my own, you know?"

"I know."

"Things are going to change," I continue. "They have to. But I don't want to give this up. I know you don't think it's important, but it's important to *me*."

We stop at a red light, and Jenn turns in her seat to face me. "I know it's important," she says. "And I don't blame you for wanting to make it work. But, April . . . I don't think it's going to."

I frown. "Wait, but I thought—I thought you just said you aren't going to make me do this alone?"

"It's not about me *making* you do anything," Jenn says. "Some people just . . . they're not *good*, you know?"

"But I *am* good," I insist. I take a deep breath. I didn't want to tell her this, but it looks like I'm going to have to. "Listen, don't tell anyone, but there's a USC rep coming to watch me play at our first game. And if they like what they see—"

"Hold on," Jenn says. "USC? What are you talking about?"

"Soccer," I say. "There's a representative from USC—probably one of the assistant coaches—coming to watch me play, and if they like what they see, they'll consider giving me a scholarship." I frown. "What are *you* talking about?"

"You and Eric," she says. "I'm saying it's not going to work out between you."

I stare at her, stunned.

"I'm not trying to be mean," Jenn says. "What I said in the boat about him being with a lot of girls . . . I'm sorry, but that's true. And, look, it doesn't make him a bad person necessarily, but I still worry you're going to get hurt. That's why you should consider ending this now, before I move." She reaches for my hand. "I don't want to worry about you and how it's going when I'm gone, you know?"

The light turns green, and Jenn takes her hand away and turns her attention back to the road. I turn away too, just as tears begin rolling down my cheeks. I finally tell her about USC—the one thing I thought would force her to really *listen* to me—and just as I feared, she didn't care at all. And if that wasn't bad enough, she's pushing me to end things with Eric so *she* can go off to college worry-free. Because who cares if I break things off with a guy I like? The real tragedy would be Jenn having to take a minute out of her day to wonder if I'm okay once she goes to college.

I wipe my eyes. I was stupid for thinking Jenn was going to take pity on me and stay around LA to help. If she cared about me and my future, she never would have lied in the first place. But this doesn't mean I'm going to give up on getting her to postpone Stanford. Hell, no. If anything, I'm even more determined. That's what makes me so good on the field, and it's what's going to help me power through this disappointment and get back on track. I'm just going to have to take a different approach, because the last ten minutes have made it clear that a straightforward attack isn't going to work.

I'm going to have to do this like Jenn would.

I'm going to have to lie.

Ten minutes later, Jenn pulls up to the curb across the street from our duplex. I take off my seat belt. "Be right back."

"Wait, we're not finished?" she asks, her hand halfway to her own seat belt. "I thought you said you wanted to go home."

"Yeah, to change," I say, careful to keep my voice light. If Jenn is going to treat me like an inconvenience, then I don't have to feel even a little bit bad about manipulating her. "Give me five minutes."

I climb out of the car and go inside. The house is dark and, for once, blissfully silent. I head upstairs, pulling my dirty clothes off as I go. One sniff of my bare arm tells me I can't just change; I need to shower. I glance out the window at the top of the stairs and see Jenn slumped down in her seat, texting. I said five minutes, but ten won't kill her. I've waited three times longer than that for her to get out of the bathroom in the morning.

I've just turned off the water and stepped out of the shower when a door slams somewhere in the house. I guess Jenn got tired of waiting in the car. I wrap the towel around myself and reach for the bathroom door, when I hear my Mom's voice coming from down the hall.

"I can't tell him that, Harriet! He'll just get upset."

Crap. It's never a good sign when Mom talks to her sister. Harriet lives in Spain, so it's hard to schedule calls with the time difference, plus they don't get along well in the first place, so when they're on the phone it means something is wrong.

"I'm just so tired of having to defend myself," Mom says. Her voice sounds strained, like she's trying not to cry. "He's always on edge, and I know I am too, but sometimes I just wish . . ." She trails off, and my heart clenches in my chest. I don't want to know what Mom wishes, but I can guess . . . and it scares the shit out of me.

"I don't know what we'd do without Jenn," Mom says. "Let's put it that way."

My sympathy hardens into something ugly and angry. If

she knew what Jenn has been keeping from her and Dad for the last few months, I doubt Mom would be talking about her like that—like she's some kind of savior and saint rolled into one.

"I know," Mom says, "but for now things need to stay the way they are. Especially since April is, well . . . *April*."

April is April? What the hell is that *supposed to mean?*

"Yes, Harriet," Mom says, her voice laced with frustration. "I *know* it's hard to be the youngest. I'm younger than you, remember? But April is almost seventeen, and she still sometimes acts like—she's just not as mature as Jenn was at her age, that's all."

I jerk back from the door. I don't want to hear any more. It's bad enough *suspecting* that my parents don't think I'm as smart or mature as my sister, but hearing it confirmed . . . how am I supposed to look them in the eye knowing that's how they feel?

The floor creaks as Mom walks down the hall and comes to a stop on the other side of the bathroom door. "It's not that I want her to be like Jenn," she says, her voice exasperated now. "That's not fair. It's just that, if she's going to grow up and have a successful life, she's going to need to do more than just hang out with her friends all the time. She's got to *do* something."

That's it—I've had enough. I trade my towel for the floral robe on the back of the door and step into the hall. Mom freezes at the sight of me.

"You scared me," she says, clutching her chest. "I didn't know anyone was home."

I cross my arms but don't answer.

"Harriet?" she says into the phone, "I have to call you back. Yes. Okay. Bye."

She slips her phone into her back pocket and smiles. "How are you, sweetie?"

"I'm fine. Immature and doomed to have a horrible future, apparently, but otherwise *just fine*."

Mom's face goes pale.

"What's funny," I continue, "is that you feel so certain about my future when you don't even know what the hell is going on in my present."

"What do you mean? Are you in trouble?"

"No!" I say, balling my hands into fists at my side. "I mean if you were paying attention, you'd know that I'm already taking care of my future! That's why soccer—"

"Soccer is not a future," Mom interrupts. "Soccer is a hobby."

"Not if I get a scholarship."

Her face falls. "Sweetie, those are very difficult to get. You have to be very good—"

My eyes fill with tears so fast I don't even realize it's happening until it's too late. Suddenly, I'm not just yelling at my mom. I'm yelling at Jenn, too. "I *am* good. I'm really good. Which you'd know if you ever paid any attention." I swipe at the tears rolling down my cheeks, but they won't stop coming. "It probably wouldn't matter anyway, though, right? Nothing I do is ever going to be enough for you and Dad. 'Cause like you said—I'm not *Jenn*."

"April, that's not what I meant—"

I stride past her into my bedroom and slam the door behind me. Mom remains in the hall, and for a few seconds I think she's going to say something.

Instead, she walks away.

CHAPTER 14

JENN

I squint across the street at the house, trying to catch a glimpse of April in her bedroom window. What is taking her so long?

When she climbed out of the car twenty minutes ago, I was tempted to follow her inside and tell her I wanted to call the rest of the day off. I already told Katie and Shruthi I'd meet them for lunch, and besides, the last few hours are surely enough to fulfill the spirit of the pact. But then Mom came home, and going inside wasn't an option. I'm lucky she was too busy talking on the phone to notice me loitering across the street. I can't put off telling her and Dad about Stanford much longer, but I'm definitely not ready to do it right now, no matter how many times Grandma texts me.

I drum my fingers on the steering wheel. What if Mom asks April where I am? Or worse, what if April rats me out and tells her I'm leaving tomorrow? She tried to put on a happy face when she was getting out of the car, but she's clearly still upset that I don't think she should be with Eric. Or maybe that I wasn't excited about somebody from USC coming to watch her play. I'll admit that I might not have taken that as seriously as I should have, though in my defense, she brought it up out of nowhere. Either way, neither of those things should be enough to make her tattle . . . right?

I need a distraction. I pick up my phone and try Tom's number again. It rings and rings, then goes to voicemail. I hang up, and check the time—it's already 12:30. There's no *way* he hasn't seen my missed calls by now.

I dial again.

Hello, you have reached Thomas Albert—

This time I wait out the end of the message. Tom hates checking his voicemail, but desperate times call for obnoxious measures.

"Hi, Tom," I say after the beep, "it's me. I've been trying to reach you all day, but I guess you're busy." I clear my throat. "Um . . . I'm having a goodbye lunch with Shruthi and Katie at the Culver City In-N-Out at two. I know we're having dinner tonight, but I hope you'll come for a little while. That way you can say goodbye to them." I hesitate, unsure how to conclude my message. I want to ask him if he's screening my calls, but if he *isn't*, I'll look paranoid. So I settle for neutral. "Okay, see you later. Bye."

I hang up just as the front door opens and April comes flying down the sidewalk, her wet curls soaking into her shirt. Of *course* she kept me waiting here while she showered. Of course.

"Switch seats!" she calls out as she nears the car.

I reluctantly climb out and head for the other side, my mind still on Tom. If he's ignoring me, I need to know why. We're leaving for Stanford tomorrow, and we can't be in a fight on the first day of our new lives together. If he doesn't make it to In-N-Out, I'll have to ask him outright when I see him at dinner tonight. Assuming we're still having dinner.

April honks the horn from inside the car. "Hurry up," she calls through the window. "We don't have all day."

The concrete steps of the Culver City Stairs carve a path up the side of the grassy, sunburnt hill. I tilt my head back and squint, but the top is out of sight.

"Ready to climb?" April asks as she gets out of the car to join me.

There are a lot of people in this world who would give anything to spend an afternoon on a hillside in Southern California, but I am not one of them. "Absolutely not."

"Oh, come on!" she says. "The view from the top is gorgeous. You can see the Santa Monica Mountains."

"You can see those from the ground."

April puts her hands on her hips. "You're moving away from Los Angeles for the next four years, right? This is your last chance to see this kind of view. It might also be a good opportunity to just slow down and . . . reflect . . . on things."

"*Reflect on things?*" I ask. "Who are you, Oprah?"

April starts to walk back around to her side of the car.

"*Fine,*" I say, pulling her back. "But we have to go slow."

She grabs a water bottle from the car, and we begin to climb. The steps are far apart and uneven, and my calves start to burn almost immediately. April makes it look easy, like she's going up the stairs of our two-story duplex, but I struggle to keep up.

"I saw Mom at home," April says.

My heart rate speeds up in my chest. I *knew* leaving April alone with Mom was a bad idea. "And?"

"She was talking to Aunt Harriet about Dad."

"Oh," I say, relieved.

"*Oh? That's bad*, Jenn. You know she only talks to Aunt Harriet when she's upset." She glances over her shoulder at me. "Something is going on with them."

"That's what they do, April. They fight." *Which you'd know if you ever bothered to pay attention to anyone other than yourself.*

"Right," she says. "But it's getting worse. I'm kind of worried."

Guilt stirs inside me. I don't want her to worry. I also know, deep down, that she's right. They've fought for years, but it's gotten worse. It started out just silly squabbles from time to time, but now it's a constant argument, from the moment they wake up till the moment they go to sleep. I don't know if it's because they don't work well together or because they're tired of being together all the time or if it's something else, but it doesn't take a therapist to know they're headed for something really, really bad.

But that's not my problem. It *can't* be. I decided a long

time ago that once I left for Stanford, that was it. I was going to distance myself—not just from their constant battles, but from worrying about them too. It's the only way to have my own life. It's the only way to be happy.

We keep climbing, the midday sun beating down on us. Sweat drips down my lower back, and my jeans start to stick to me. I pull my cardigan off and tie it around my waist, but it doesn't help.

"Can we stop for a second?" I ask, breathing hard. "I just need a little break."

April sighs.

"I'm sorry we can't all be superathletes," I grumble as I massage my thigh. I look up the hill and my stomach sinks. The Stairs go on *forever*. "How many steps are there?"

"Um, I don't know?" she says, not meeting my eye.

"April, tell me how many there are or I'm going back to the car."

"Okay, fine," she says. "There are two hundred and eighty-two. But they go by really fast."

"Two *hundred* and eighty-two?"

"It's not that many," April insists. "I climb them all the time."

"I'm sorry, but I don't want to do this. I'm going back down."

April gapes at me. "Are you serious? We've already come so far!"

"And we have even farther to go."

She shakes her head. "I can't believe this. I came up with

this whole day for you, picked all this stuff you'd like, and you've complained about every single place we've gone."

"What about this seems like something *I'd* like?" I demand. "You're the one who does outdoorsy things, not me. If this were for me, we'd be—"

"In a library?" April cuts in. "Sounds really fun."

I glare at her. "How would you know? It's not like you ever spend any time there. You barely even read."

I regret the words before they're all the way out of my mouth, but I know it's too late to take them back. April looks like she's about to reply, but someone clears their throat, and we both turn. Four steps below us, a guy in a tank top and shorts is staring at us, a look on his face that says he heard every word. "Excuse me," he says. "Can I get by . . . ?"

We both step to the side, and he climbs past us. As soon as he's gone, April turns away from me and crosses her arms.

"I'm sorry," I say. "That was mean."

"Yeah," April says, not turning around. "It was."

I climb the few steps to where she's standing and gently put my hand on her shoulder. "We have more stops ahead of us, right?"

She moves out from under my hand and turns around. "Right."

"And we've already wasted a bunch of time going to the impound and back home so you could change—"

"Those stops were both *your* fault," she says. "Not mine."

"Fine, fine," I say, holding up my hands in surrender. "You're right. But the fact remains that the day is already halfway over, and while you can run up these stairs in ten minutes, it's going to take me forever to get to the top. I'll probably have to stop . . . five times?"

"At least," she says. "You're not in climbing shape."

"Hey!" I exclaim. "Rude, much?"

"Sorry," she says quickly. "I wasn't talking about your weight. It's just that this sort of thing is highly aerobic, which means—"

I hold up a hand. "I know what 'aerobic' means. I took AP Bio, thank you."

"They teach that in PE, too, you know," she says. "But yeah, at this rate we won't get to the top any time soon, and I'm already kind of hungry."

I consider telling her about the change of lunch plans, but she's looking at me like she wants to push me down the stairs, so I decide to wait. "Okay then," I say. "Should we leave?"

"Oh, we're not giving up," April says, starting back down the stairs. "We're just going to find another way to the top."

CHAPTER 15

APRIL

What's the point of climbing the steps if you can just drive up here?" Jenn asks as we pull into a parking spot at the top of the hill.

I get out of the car, not bothering to answer her. I'm too busy thinking about what Jenn said on the stairs, about me barely reading. It was a low blow, but it was also total bullshit. Just because I don't ace every single class doesn't mean I don't love books. I've listened to dozens of audiobooks in the last year, most of the time while I'm on my morning runs, and *I'm* the one who insisted Mom read Harry Potter to us when we were kids. But I can't let Jenn's judgmental crap get in the way of what I'm here to do. If anything it makes convincing her to stay in LA even more important, since the only way to prove to her that I'm not some dumb jock without a future is by getting that scholarship to USC. And the only way to do *that* is to keep her here in LA, working at the store.

I start across the parking lot, leaving Jenn to hurry after

me. Our visit to the Stairs isn't *technically* inspired by a photo or a childhood memory like the rest of our stops, but I thought she'd like it anyway. It's a classic LA thing to do, and it's one of the places I'd miss if I were about to abandon my family. In retrospect, making her sweat her way up a hill wasn't the best way to convince her not to leave, but the view she's about to see from the top? Between the ocean to the west, downtown LA to the east, and the Santa Monica Mountains in the distance, it's a showstopper. There's no way it won't make her rethink her plans.

Jenn gets out of the car, and we walk across the parking lot to the overlook and gaze down at the city below us.

Or we try to. Unfortunately, there's so much smog hanging in the distance above downtown, the whole scene is kinda hazy. Definitely not the kind of view to inspire someone to put off going away to college for a year. *Shit.*

"Wow," Jenn says.

"Yeah," I mutter. "It's kind of polluted."

"True. But it reminds me of the view from the roof of our house."

I look at her in surprise. "Really?"

"Yeah! It's similar to this, except, you know, not from quite so high up. We used to go up there all the time, remember?"

I grin. "I'd pretend it was my bedroom, and you'd pretend—"

"That I was Wonder Woman," Jenn says, laughing. "So lame."

"More like so awesome," I say, nudging her.

She smiles. "Should we take a picture?"

I reach for my phone, but she pulls hers out first. "This way I can keep it when I leave."

My smile falters, but Jenn leans toward me, and I hitch it back up just in time for the photo.

As Jenn checks her text messages, I look at Culver City stretching before us and think back to when we first went up onto the roof. We'd only been living in the building for a few weeks when I realized our duplex even had roof access. Well, not *official* access, but if you climbed out the window, you stepped right onto the roof, and that was basically the same thing. At first I didn't tell Jenn because I wanted it to be a secret, but then I realized secrets are only fun if you can share them with someone. Plus, it was boring up there by myself. So late one night we put on our pajamas, grabbed a Ouija board, and headed outside. We ended up falling asleep out there and sneaking back in when the sun came up. Miraculously, Mom and Dad never found out. After that, we did it at least once a month. I don't actually know why we stopped.

"Remember when we brought up sparkling cider and pretended it was champagne?" Jenn asks. "We thought we were so fancy."

"We *were* fancy," I say. "We were wearing the new dresses Mom had bought us for Aunt Sharon's neighbor's bat mitzvah."

"Mom was furious when she saw all the dirt on my butt." Jenn shakes her head. "It's been a long time since I've been up on that roof. I bet it's a mess now."

"It was a mess back then, too, and it didn't matter."

"True."

I look at her out of the corner of my eye. "We could go up there again, you know. We could probably even get our hands on some *real* champagne. Or at least some cheap beer."

"Totally," she says, but the smile quickly slips off her face. "I mean, if I come back for the holidays. I'm probably going to be pretty busy, and my new roommate already invited me to stay in town with her family for Thanksgiving, so . . ."

Anger floods through me, so fast it catches me by surprise. Not visiting over Thanksgiving break? Is she really that done with our family?

"Thanks for doing all this," she says suddenly, gesturing around us. "I'm really glad I get to see this before I go."

I smile tightly. "Sure."

"To be honest," she says, "I thought you were mad at me after our conversation in the car. I was actually worried."

"That I was upset?"

"No, that you were going to tell Mom about Stanford when they came home earlier."

"You thought I'd *tattle* on you?"

"It's not like you've been particularly mature about this whole thing, April."

I hug my knees to my chest. First mom says I'm immature, now Jenn is doing it too. And yet *neither* of them knows a damn thing about me. It's not fair.

"Anyway," she goes on, "I'm glad we did this. All of it. It's been a really nice way to spend my last day before I leave. It's helping me feel more ready to move on." She sighs. "Mom and Dad are going to be pissed, but sometimes you've got to do what feels right, you know?"

"Totally," I say, forcing myself to smile. "I mean, this is your life, right? You should do whatever you want. Who cares what other people think or feel?"

She narrows her eyes, but I keep going. I'm done playing nice. If Jenn is this selfish, then she deserves it. "It's gotta be hard to walk away from your entire life, though," I say. "All your friends."

She looks unsure. "A little, I guess."

"Shruthi and Katie are staying here, right?" I ask.

"Yep. UCLA."

"They're going to college together too?" *This is it. This is how I get her to stay.* "Aren't you worried they might . . . I don't know, forget about you?"

Jenn frowns. "Why would they forget about me? It's not like I'm never coming back. And we can still talk on the phone."

"Sure, but that's not the same thing."

She crosses her arms, and I realize she wants to walk away. I don't blame her. But if that's how she's feeling, then that means this is working. She's rethinking her plans.

"It's also kind of strange," I press, "that they didn't want to hang out with you today. I mean, you're leaving—"

"Oh, speaking of that," Jenn says, "they actually asked me if I wanted to have a late lunch as a kind of farewell, so after we're done here I'm going to meet them."

"Wait, you're ditching me?"

"Oh, you can totally come," she says, in that special tone reserved for telling someone they are *welcome* when they're anything but. "I'm sure they wouldn't mind."

"But I thought *we* were having lunch together."

"Is it really that big of a deal? We've been together all day."

I turn away from her, as much to hide my own face as to avoid looking at hers. A stupid goodbye lunch with Jenn's friends is *not* part of the plan. But that's not all that bothers me. She knew I came up with activities for us to do all day, *and* I stayed out with her even after she knocked me into the freaking canal and got our car towed. And yet she still agreed behind my back to ditch me for her friends. I know my sister and I aren't close, but that doesn't mean she should treat me like an afterthought.

Whatever. It's going to take more than a passive-aggressive lunch date to make me give up on convincing Jenn to stay in LA.

"I'll go," I say, "but I want to invite Nate."

"Fine. Tell him we're meeting at In-N-Out on Washington in"—she checks the time—"twenty minutes."

"*Fine,*" I say back, even though I know it makes me sound like a brat. "I will."

Jenn pulls her cell phone out of her purse, unaware of the war I'm raging against her. "I'm going to call Tom while you do that. Meet you back at the car?"

She walks away, leaving me gazing over the city alone. When I woke up this morning, everything made sense. Jenn was going to college in LA and working at the store, Eric and I were doing great, and I was working toward a scholarship. Now Eric is mad at me, I might have to drop out of soccer, and all I've succeeded in doing is driving Jenn even further away from me than she was when the day started.

At least she seemed truly upset about the idea of her friends moving on without her once she goes to Stanford. Maybe seeing them at lunch will change her mind about moving away. Nothing I say will make Jenn stay—she's made it clear that I don't matter. But maybe she'll stay for her friends. I've done everything else I can think of to convince her, so I might as well try this, too.

I have to believe there's still a way to fix this. I don't have a choice.

CHAPTER 16

JENN

The parking lot at In-N-Out smells amazing, like cheeseburgers and fries and the end of summer. It reminds me of all the times I've come here, first with my parents when I was too little to eat an entire hamburger on my own, then later with April, when we'd save up money and walk over on the weekends. Then a few years later, my friends and I would swing by after school, so Katie could have something to eat before her evening dance classes across town. I'm hit with a pang of homesickness, so sudden and thorough that it stops me in my tracks even though it doesn't make any sense—I haven't even left home yet, and it's not like they don't have In-N-Out in Northern California. But it sends me reeling just the same.

"You okay?" April asks.

"I'm fine," I say, waving her off. "Just tired."

"Hi!" Shruthi says when we step inside. She throws her arms around me, and I'm enveloped by the gentle scent of her peony perfume. It simultaneously makes me feel better and much, much worse.

"I cannot believe this is the last time we're going to see you," Shruthi says into my hair. "I'm going to miss you so much."

"It's the last time we're going to see her *until Thanksgiving*," Katie corrects from a few feet away. "Don't be dramatic." But as soon as Shruthi steps back, Katie tosses her long blond ponytail over her shoulder and hugs me too.

"Hi, April," Shruthi says after the hugs are over. "How are you?"

"I'm fine," April says, not making eye contact with her. "Have you seen Nate?"

"Nope," Shruthi says, her voice kind despite how rude April is being. "Do you want to wait for him, or should we get in line?"

"Let's order," April says. "I know what he likes anyway."

Five minutes later, we grab our drinks and Katie leads us toward a booth in the corner. We take our seats—Katie and Shruthi on one side, April and I on the other.

"It's really nice of you to organize an entire day for your sister," Shruthi says when we're settled. "My sister would never do that. She's a total brat."

"Your sister's only six!" Katie says.

"Doesn't mean she isn't a brat."

"Why *did* you do it?" Katie asks April. "Was it a going-away present?"

We all look at April, and for the second time today, I'm

nervous about what she's going to say. Will she remind them she couldn't give me a going-away present because she hadn't known I was going away in the first place? That she never would have organized today if she had? I doubt Katie and Shruthi would blame her. In fact, they'd probably be pissed at me, since I *might* have led them to believe I'd come clean weeks ago, just to keep them off my back.

But April doesn't say any of these things. Instead, she slides out of the booth. "I'll be right back. I'm gonna call Nate and find out if he's coming."

When she's gone, Shruthi turns to me. "Are you ready for tomorrow?"

"I think so," I say. "Tom's picking me up at seven. The flight's only an hour, so we should be on campus before lunch."

"Where is Tom, anyway?" Katie asks. "Did you ever get him on the phone?"

I pull the wrapper off my straw and wind it around my finger. "No."

"Hmm," Shruthi says, and looks at Katie. "She's got that face."

"What face?" I say. "I don't have a face."

Katie snorts. "She's totally got that face."

"*What* face?"

"Whenever you're hiding how you feel about something, you get this look," Shruthi explains. "Your lips get kinda thin, and this crease shows up between your eyes—"

I drop my straw wrapper and touch my forehead. "Oh my god."

Katie picks up the fallen wrapper and throws it at me. "Dude, you're too young for wrinkles. But she's right. You're totally freaking out."

I pick up my straw wrapper again. "I still haven't heard from him. It's starting to make me nervous."

"He's probably just busy with his family," Shruthi says. "It's his last day with them."

"Or his phone is dead," Katie says. "Tessa's phone is always dying."

Shruthi and I glance at each other, but don't say anything. Katie has been dating Tessa on and off for years, but we're both hoping Tessa going to University of Michigan will flip the switch to *off* permanently.

"I really don't think you need to worry about Tom," Shruthi says. "But you should go to his house after lunch. Talk face-to-face."

"Maybe," I say. "We're going to a sushi place in the Marina that we like, so I guess I can just ask him then."

"Wait, you're having dinner with him instead of your family?" Shruthi says. "My grandma would *kill* me."

"My parents would too," Katie says.

I crumple my straw wrapper into a ball and don't answer. Mom and Dad are the last people I want to spend my last night with.

Shruthi's phone buzzes. "Katie, look!" she exclaims. "That blue rug is back in stock at West Elm! I just got the notification."

They bend over Shruthi's phone, and Katie fist pumps.

"It's even on sale! We're going to have the cutest dorm room ever."

"Wait—you're living together?" I ask. "I didn't know that."

Katie looks up from Shruthi's phone. "We told you months ago."

"No, you didn't."

"Really? I could have sworn we told you in the group chat." She looks at Shruthi. "Didn't we?"

"Maybe we just talked about it in our private text."

I frown. "Since when do you have one of those?"

"I think we started it when we both got into UCLA. We didn't want to bother you with all the details."

"It wouldn't have bothered me."

Katie snorts. "Dude, *everything* about college bothered you. For months."

"It's true," Shruthi says gently. "We tried talking to you about it a million times, but you got all distant every time it came up." She looks at Katie. "We've been worried about you."

"Then why didn't you say something?" I know I sound angry, but I can't help it. "That's what friends are supposed to do. They're supposed to be honest with each other."

Katie scoffs. "Give me a break. You are the *last* person who should be lecturing us about honesty. You didn't tell your own *parents* you were going to college."

"That's different—"

"Stop," Shruthi says, holding up a hand. "This is our last

lunch together. We are not going to spend it arguing."

Katie and I continue staring at each other, but when an embarrassed flush starts to creep over my cheeks, I look away. Shruthi is right. We shouldn't be arguing, not when we have so little time left together. I can't help but be pissed, though. Not just at Katie, but at *both* of them.

"Jenn, I think your food is ready," Shruthi says, nodding toward the counter. "They just called your number."

"Oh. Thanks." I hop up, and head for the counter. Three trays—mine, April's, and Nate's—are sitting side by side. I grab them and head back to the table. Katie and Shruthi are leaning toward each other, Katie's blond hair against Shruthi's brown, and they're whispering. My insides immediately freeze up.

"I'm going to take this out to April," I announce. "Be right back."

I turn on my heel and head outside, April's question running through my head. Could they really be moving on without me?

CHAPTER 17

APRIL

I find Nate outside, seated at a picnic table under a big umbrella. I'm about to join him, when I realize he's on the phone.

"I know, Mom," he says in a tone that suggests he's said these same words at least twice already. "I have to go, okay? April's waiting for me inside." He's silent for a second, then nods. "Okay. I'll tell her. Yes, I promise. Okay. Bye."

"Tell me what?" I say, sitting down next to him.

He shoves his phone into his pocket. "She wants you to come over for dinner next week. She's making Galbi-jjim."

"My favorite," I say. "Tell her to name the night, and I'm there."

"She always makes a ton, so chances are you could come on any given night and that's what we'll be having."

The door to the patio opens, and Jenn steps outside, three plastic In-N-Out trays in her hands. "Oh," she says. "You're here."

"Am I not supposed to be?" Nate asks.

"No, no, I just meant—never mind."

Jenn places two trays on the table in front of us, the burgers bumping against one another before falling over.

Nate and I glance at each other. "Are you angry at me or something?" I ask.

"No, I just wanted to talk."

"Okay . . ." I start to stand, but Jenn shakes her head.

"It's fine. You guys can stay here."

"But we're supposed to be having lunch together," I say. "We were just about to come inside."

"I know," she says, looking back over her shoulder toward the door, "but maybe I should . . ."

My heart gives an unexpected squeeze in my chest. I'm not used to seeing Jenn like this, and I have a feeling it has to do with what I said back at the Stairs. I should be pleased, since making her regret her decision to leave is exactly what I set out to do, but instead I feel like a total asshole.

"It's okay if you want to have lunch with your friends," I say. "We can hang out after."

"Are you sure?" She looks hesitant, almost like she doesn't want me to say yes. It makes me feel even worse.

"If you want to," I say. "Or you can stay here. It's up to you."

She bites her lip. "No, I should go in. I'll see you later."

She heads inside, and I watch her cross the room to where her friends are waiting for her with their food.

"What the hell is going on?" Nate asks. "Why is she being so weird?"

I pick up a french fry, then put it back down again. "I may have said something that's making her a little . . . paranoid."

"Like what?"

I look down at my hands. "I told her if she leaves, her friends are going to forget about her."

"*What?*" Nate says. "Why would you say that?"

"Because I don't want her to leave! If she does, our parents are going to implode, and I'll have to work at the store after school, which means *goodbye, soccer,* and . . . she just has to stay. She *has* to."

We sit there silently, neither of us eating. Then Nate puts his arm around me. "The bad news is that it's very unlikely that you will be successful in convincing her to stay."

I groan. "What's the good news?"

He hands me my double-double. "You're at In-N-Out."

I laugh weakly and take a bite. The *burgercheesebunsauce* combination practically melts in my mouth, and I have to admit—it makes me feel a tiny bit better.

"Who doesn't tell their family about going away to college?" Nate asks suddenly. "I've been thinking about it all day, and I just don't get it."

"I asked her the same thing this morning, and she basically told me to mind my own business."

Nate shakes his head. "I don't know, dude. I've worked with Jenn at the store for almost a year, and this isn't like her. I wonder if something else happened."

The idea that Nate could have some kind of insight into my sister that I don't sends a jolt of jealousy through me I wasn't expecting. "What could have happened that would make her lie to us?"

He takes a bite of his burger, chews slowly, and swallows. "Maybe something with your parents."

I put my burger down. "Like what?"

"Dunno, but they're pretty rough on her."

"Oh, come on, she's the golden child."

His face hardens. "That's not always the easiest thing to be."

I watch him for a second, waiting for him to say more, but instead he crumples up a napkin and says, "Anyway—"

"No 'anyway,'" I say. "We're clearly not talking about Jenn anymore, and something has been going on with you since this morning. I want to know what it is."

He grimaces. "I don't know what you mean."

"BS, Nate. First you're on edge in the kitchen—and don't tell me it was just about Eric—and then you say something is up with your family. Then you tell me your mom is on your case, and now you say it's hard being the golden child."

He shifts uncomfortably. "I really don't want to talk about this right now, okay? I promise I will eventually, but this is the first time all day my mom hasn't been texting or calling me, and I just want to eat this burger in peace."

"Fine," I say. "But this isn't over. We're going to talk about this, even if I have to sit on your back like I used to do when we were kids."

"Please don't," he says. "I used to inhale so much sand that my mom thought I was developing a respiratory infection."

"I'll do whatever it takes to make you talk," I say in my best gangster voice. Nate rolls his eyes. "Now, what were we talking about again?"

"College," he says.

"Oh, right. So what about you? Do you think you'll go away for school?"

"Mom wants me to stay local—"

"But what do *you* want?"

"I want to go wherever you go," he says immediately.

My face floods with heat, and for a second I don't know what to do. We're best friends, so him wanting to go to college together shouldn't surprise me. But the way he said that just now, and the way he's looking at me . . . it doesn't *feel* like he's talking about going as friends.

Nate clears his throat. "What about you? Still planning on becoming the next Alyssa Naeher?"

I look at him in surprise. "How do you know who Alyssa Naeher is?"

"I *may* have started watching women's soccer over the summer."

"What! Why?"

"I guess I got tired of listening to you talk about it all the time but never understanding what the hell you were saying. Plus . . ." He scrunches up his face. "Never mind, it's stupid."

"You *know* you're not allowed to 'never mind' me," I scold. "Come on, tell me."

He fiddles with his burger wrapper. "You and Eric."

"What about us?"

"You guys both play soccer, and now that you're on varsity, you're going to be spending even more time together."

"It's not like we're on the same team," I say. "We don't even practice on the same field."

"I know," he says. "But it's still going to happen. Which is fine, don't get me wrong. I just don't want you to, I don't know . . . forget about me."

My breath catches in my chest. I know Eric and Nate don't get along—and after what he said in the car, I suspect it's mostly Eric's fault—but Nate's never sounded worried about what us dating would mean for our friendship before.

"I'm not going to forget about you," I say. "No matter what."

We look at each other, and for the first time, I can't read his expression. Whatever this moment is, we need to get out of it and back to neutral territory. Because the urge I have to take his hand and *also* run in the opposite direction at the same time? It is *not* working for me.

"There's one thing you should know if you're going to become a soccer fan," I say, my voice serious. "It's *crucial*, really."

"What's that?" he asks, his mouth quirking into a smile.

"If you leave the United States," I say, "don't call it 'soccer.' You've gotta say 'football.' Especially if you're in the UK. Otherwise, you'll probably get jumped by a hooligan."

"A hooli-*what*?" he says. "You know what? Never mind."

We finish our food a few minutes later, then head inside. Jenn's burger is barely half-gone, but Katie and Shruthi's side of the table is strewn with burger wrappers and cold french fries.

"There you are!" Katie says when she sees us walking over. Her voice is oddly cheerful, like she's trying to cover for something. "I thought you were going to eat with us."

I glance at Jenn, but she doesn't meet my eye. "Sorry," I say to Katie, "we got distracted."

Jenn scoots in so I can join her side of the booth. Nate grabs a chair and sits at the end.

"So, Nate," Shruthi says. "Are you ready for junior year?"

We start to talk about what classes we're taking, which chem teachers will let you watch *Breaking Bad* for extra credit, and why it's worth taking the PSAT first even if you're doing well on at-home practice tests. I try to listen, but I keep thinking about what Nate said about going to college together. He tried to play it off like it wasn't a big deal, but the way he said it . . .

Across the table, Nate winks at me, and I realize I've been staring at him.

Suddenly, I feel warm. No, not warm—*hot*. I excuse myself from the table and head to the bathroom. Once there, I soak a paper towel with cold water and press it to my forehead. What is *wrong* with me?

The door swings open, and my sister comes in. "You okay?" she asks. "You got really red all of a sudden."

I throw away the wet paper towel and grab another to dry my face. "I'm fine."

"If you say so." She opens one of the stalls but doesn't go inside. "Thanks again for being cool with me sitting with my friends. I know you wanted it to be just us."

I don't say anything, because the truth is, I did want that . . . but not for the right reasons.

"So where were we going to go?" she asks. "If it had been only us?"

"Tito's Tacos."

Jenn's mouth drops open. "Are you serious? I *hate* Tito's, April. You know that."

I turn around to face her, so my back is against the sink. "No, you don't. We had your thirteenth birthday party there. Remember, Mom made that huge cake?"

"Yeah, and did you ever think about *why* she made such a huge cake if it was only for the four of us?"

"No?"

"Because we invited my entire seventh-grade class even though we had just moved to the district, and *no one else showed up*. It was humiliating."

The thought of Jenn feeling that way—because of something our parents did, no less—throws me for a loop. I've always thought of the three of them as being completely in sync. But there's another piece of this that cuts even deeper— that the party had nothing to do with me.

"I thought you only wanted to celebrate with me," I say, my cheeks flushing, "and that's why no one else was there. But I guess that's pretty stupid in retrospect."

"It's not stupid," Jenn says quietly. "It's just not true."

The door swings open, and a woman and her young son come inside. "Sorry," she says, "but he has to go and my husband is on the phone."

"Look," Jenn says once the woman and her son are inside the stall, "I'm not mad, okay? It's just, I'm about to move, so the last thing I want to think about is how much it sucked being the new kid with zero friends, you know? It's bad enough that my current friends are already moving on without me."

"Jenn, I shouldn't have said that—"

Jenn's phone buzzes. "It's Mom," she says, checking the screen. "They need us to cover the store for an hour while they run an errand."

I roll my eyes. "Can't you just tell them we're busy or something?"

"I can't *refuse* to go, April."

"Why not?"

Jenn stares at me like I'm out of my mind. "Because it's not right to shirk responsibility like that."

"You aren't shirking responsibility if it isn't your shift. And besides, we're not done with the pact. We still have a few more stops."

Jenn rubs her temples. "To be honest, I'm kind of tired. I appreciate everything you've done for me today, but I just want to go see what they need, get it over with, and go home."

So that's it, then. Not only has my plan failed miserably, but she doesn't even want to hang out with me anymore. "Okay," I say. "Sure."

"Thanks," Jenn says, pulling open the door. "See you out there."

CHAPTER 18

JENN

We head toward the car, sodas in hand. The sun is high in the sky above us, baking down on the top of my head. Shruthi and Katie wave goodbye from across the parking lot, but I pretend not to notice.

"When are you going to tell Mom and Dad?" April asks the moment we're in the car.

I wrap my fingers around the steering wheel, ignoring the way the hot leather heats my palms. It's a fair question—one Grandma has asked me at least once a week since I got into Stanford—but the thought of seeing their faces fills me with dread. I check the time on the dash. Three o'clock. There's still time.

I start the car. "I'll tell them later."

"Don't you think maybe you should tell them *now*?" April says. "You're kind of running out of time—"

"You don't think I know that?" I snap. "Put your seat belt on."

I reverse out of the space and edge my way toward the exit. Beside me, April shakes her head.

"I still don't understand why you kept it from them in the first place."

I turn on the AC, then roll my windows down for good measure. "That's because you have no clue what it's like dealing with Mom and Dad," I say. "You have the perfect relationship with them."

April chokes on her soda. "I'm sorry—*what*?"

"You run around doing whatever you want, totally oblivious, and then you come home and lock yourself in your room. Mom and Dad never ask you to do anything. You have no idea what it's like being in the store with them every day."

"Oh, please," April says, crossing her arms. "You love it. You get to be the golden child. Why else would you work there?"

"Because I have to." I grip the steering wheel even harder. Is she really this clueless? "If I'm not there to make them stop fighting, the whole place would shut down," I explain. "And if you haven't noticed, the store is what pays our bills."

"Wait," April says. "That's why you work there? To make them stop fighting?"

"I mean, not originally, but if I didn't the whole business would probably collapse. They're too busy verbally abusing each other to run the store properly."

April's eyes go wide. "I knew they fought a lot, but I didn't realize it was affecting their business."

We pull up to a red light, and I turn to face her. "It's not just affecting their business. It's affecting everything." I take a deep breath and let it out slowly. "Remember that night we were supposed to go to Uncle Chris's birthday party? But instead Mom and Dad got in a huge argument and we stayed home?"

April groans. "I had to go to Nate's to get away from the yelling."

"Yeah, well, it got bad. *Really* bad. They started bringing up all these old grudges, and by the end of the fight Mom was talking about divorce."

April's mouth drops open. "Really?"

"Yes," I say. "Really."

The light turns green, and I start to drive again.

"But what does that have to do with Stanford?" April asks.

I shift in my seat. If I tell her the rest of what happened that night, there's no going back. She'll know *exactly* how bad things have gotten between our parents. But maybe that's a good thing. "I got into Stanford that same day. I was going to tell them, but then everything went to hell. So I gave them the acceptance letter and went to bed. The next morning, they came into my room and told me I wasn't allowed to go away for college. They said I had to apply somewhere else. Somewhere in LA."

"But why? Why would they want you to stay . . ." Her eyes go wide as the truth hits her. "You think they wanted you here because otherwise they'd fight even more and eventually . . . get a divorce?"

I nod. "At the time I was too upset to think it through.

But later, when I saw how relieved they were, I realized what was really going on." My voice shakes, but I push forward. "I was so angry, but I didn't want to be the reason they got a divorce. I love them, you know? I wanted them to be happy. I still do."

"Then why are you still going?" April asks.

"Because when it came time to turn Stanford down, I couldn't do it. I didn't want to stay in LA anymore, not if nothing was going to change. So instead I talked to Grandma, and she helped me apply. And . . . that's it. You know the rest."

We pull up in front of the store, and I turn off the car. We sit in silence, watching the cars speed by. It feels strange to have told April all of that. I've kept things from her for so long that it's almost a habit, but being honest with her about how bad things are between me and Mom and Dad is a huge relief. But another feeling surfaces, one I wasn't expecting—guilt. I might not be alone anymore, but there's a new burden in being the one to tell April, because now she has to live with it. I'm sure that's scary, and painful, and a million other emotions I've grown accustomed to burying. But April deserves to know the truth. It's the only way she's going to be able to deal with them on her own for the next two years.

"I guess you're glad you don't have to worry about any of this anymore," April says suddenly.

I turn in my seat to look at her. "What do you mean?"

She nods at the store. "O'Farrell's, Mom and Dad. Our family. You don't have to care about any of it anymore."

"That's not fair," I say. "I still care about those things."

"Really?" She crosses her arms. "Because it seems like you're perfectly happy dumping all of this in my lap. So what if I have to give up soccer and—"

"Oh, I'm *so* sorry," I say, cutting her off. "*Poor* April has to actually *contribute* for once. How awful for you that you have to act like you're part of this family."

"That's bullshit," she says. "I'm constantly trying to be part of this family. Why else would I spend all day trying to make you happy even though you lied to me for *months*? Why else would I try to convince you to stay in LA?"

"Wait," I say, holding up my hand. "What did you just say? You've been trying to convince me to stay?"

The color drains from April's face. "Oh . . . um, yeah? But I didn't mean—what I was *trying* to say was—"

I narrow my eyes.

She clasps her hands in her lap. "I thought that maybe if I could convince you not to go to Stanford this year, you might, you know, not leave me alone with Mom and Dad. You might defer a year so you could stay here and help me."

"Wait, is *that* why you said Katie and Shruthi might be moving on without me?"

April flushes. "I thought maybe it'd make you stay, and then I wouldn't have to give up soccer. . . ."

The weight of what she's saying slowly sinks in. I knew she was irritated by me leaving at first, but I thought she was coming around. She *said* she understood. She even chose to stick to the pact, even after I gave her a way out. I believed she wanted to spend time with me. And when she said those horrible things about my friends, I believed *that*, too. I thought she cared about me.

But it was never about me. I was right from the beginning—my sister always has an angle. I was naïve to think any different.

"I knew you were self-centered," I say, my voice shaking, "but this is so much worse than I realized." I turn away from her and look out the window. It's the only way to keep my fury from spiraling into tears. "And for the record, there is no way I'd ever stay here. *Especially* not for you."

The car goes silent, the only noise coming from the street outside. Then she starts to cry. "I was only trying to do what was right," she says, sniffling. "For our family. That's why I tried to convince you to stay by taking you to places you love—"

"Places *I* love?" I choke out. "April, everywhere you took me today was about *you*. First the Ferris wheel, where you conveniently forgot throwing up all over me. Then Muscle Beach, where *you* once celebrated *your* achievements. Then the Stairs, which is the *last* thing I'd ever choose to do, and finally, you were going to take me to Tito's! My least-favorite restaurant *ever!*" I hit the steering wheel with the heel of my hand. "If you really wanted me to stay in LA, you would have taken me somewhere that was about *both* of us. Not just *you*." I roll my eyes. "But I bet you can't think of a single place. You're *that* selfish."

"I can too!" April says. "I could pick the perfect place if I had to. In fact, I'll prove it to you: Meet me there at eight o'clock. That should give you plenty of time to see your precious Thomas *and* to realize what an asshole you're being."

"Yeah, fine," I say, waving her off. "Whatever."

She climbs out of the car, slams the door behind her . . . and waits. I know what she's doing. She expects me to roll down the window and apologize even though she's the one who's been a complete monster. But I'm not going to. I'm done with her games. So instead I start the car, check my mirrors, and drive away, leaving her in the middle of the street, alone. She can go into the store and face Mom and Dad by herself.

It's exactly what she deserves.

CHAPTER 19

APRIL

"Mom, are you in there?" I pound on the door of O'Farrell Antiques, not caring that the glass is rattling in its frame. "Dad? Open the door!"

I wipe my eyes and step back from the door. I can't believe this. First they demand we come to the store, then Jenn abandons me, and now no one is here. If this isn't the perfect metaphor for my family, I don't know what is. I wipe my eyes again, and peer up and down the street. There's no sign of their SUV, but maybe they're parked in back.

I head around the corner to the small lot behind O'Farrell's. No SUV . . . and the back door is locked too. *Great*.

I pull out my cell phone and try calling them. It goes to voicemail. "Where are you guys?" I ask, my voice catching. "I'm here, but no one . . . no one else is." I clear my throat and will myself not to start crying again. "Call me back."

I hang up and try the door one more time, just in case. I'm about to give up—I can't just stand here all day, sweating my ass off in the sun—when I picture Jenn's smug face when she finds out I left before Mom and Dad got here. She'll say it's proof that I'm lazy and a terrible member of this family. No *way* am I giving her the opportunity. I have to find another way inside.

I walk around to the side of the building, searching for a door I don't know about, or maybe a window. Sure enough, I find a window that's cracked open and just big enough to squeeze through. The only problem is that it's about six feet off the ground. I drop my purse, then hunt around for something to stand on. Eventually, I find two milk crates in the back alley and stack them beneath the window. I climb up, plant my hands on the dirty windowsill, ignoring the way the grit immediately sticks to my palms, and heave myself up. So far so good. I push the window open the rest of the way with one hand, then start to pull myself inside.

I'm halfway through when I realize that six feet off the ground *outside* is six feet off the ground *inside*, too. Which means the moment I push myself all the way through this window, I'm going to fall face-first into the store.

Shit.

My arms start to ache from supporting myself. I take a deep breath and adjust my grip on the windowsill. I can't keep going forward, and I can't go feetfirst, either, because the window is way too small to turn around in. I have to get down and figure something else out.

Except getting down isn't easy either. I could drop back to the ground, but if I hit the milk crates beneath me on my way down, I'll screw up my ankle. And if that happens, my soccer days will be over, regardless of what my parents and Jenn think. I'm just going to have to climb back down the way I came up. I feel around for the milk crates. They should be right beneath me, but the window is so high that the toe of my shoe barely grazes the top. I reposition my hands so I can reach down a bit farther with my foot, and eventually I find the crate on top—and knock it over.

"Shit." Without the crate, I can't get down, and without being able to see where I'll land, I can't jump, either. Which means I'm stuck.

"Shit," I say again. "Shit, shit, *shit*."

"April?"

I look up. Mom and Dad are standing in the doorway to their office, staring at me from inside the store.

"What in the world are you *doing*?" Dad asks.

"Trying to get inside! The door was locked, and you guys weren't answering your phone—"

"So you decided to break into a window the size of a doggy door?" Mom says. "Why didn't you just wait?"

I try to shrug, but it's hard to do when you're holding up your entire body weight with your arms.

With Mom and Dad's help, I'm down from the window a few minutes later. I follow them inside and sit in the leather desk chair in front of their ancient desktop. "So what's up?" I ask. "What do you guys need?"

"Just wait a second," Mom says. "We have to turn on the lights so people know we're open again."

An hour later, I'm still waiting. Mom and Dad buzz around in the store, alternating between muttering to themselves and arguing in low tones as they fuss with a display near the front window. I've offered to help more than once, but each time I try, they shoo me away and tell me to be patient. I'm about to volunteer again just to have something to do, when my cell phone buzzes in my bag. I pull it out, thinking it might be my sister calling to apologize, but it's a text from Eric. I sigh with relief. I make sure my parents aren't going to choose this exact moment to finally tell me what I'm doing here, then I open the message.

Great seeing you last night. You should wear that more often ☺

Last night? I didn't see Eric last night. Which means—

My heart plummets to the bottom of my stomach. Jenn was right. He's seeing other people.

Sure enough, another text comes through almost immediately. **Sorry, wrong chat. Hope you're having fun with your sister!**

My eyes fill with tears. What did I do wrong? Until this afternoon I thought everything was going so well. Except clearly it *wasn't*, because last night he hooked up with whoever that text was meant for, probably minutes after he asked me if I could come over. How did I not see this coming? Eric's popular and hot and on the freaking soccer team. Of course I couldn't hold his interest. I toss my phone onto the desk. I'm such an idiot.

Mom comes to the office door. "April, do you know where— Are you crying?"

"No," I say, quickly wiping away my tears. "What's up?"

Mom looks unconvinced, but doesn't push. "Do you know where your sister is?"

I grind my teeth at the mention of Jenn. "Not here."

"Obviously," Dad says, joining us. "If she were, you wouldn't have come in through the back window like a poorly trained cat burglar."

"Very funny," I grumble.

"What happened?" Dad says. "I thought you were together."

"She dropped me off and left."

Mom narrows her eyes. "That's all?"

Dad leans against the doorway and crosses his arms. "April, it's not like your sister to ignore us. If she dropped you and left after we specifically asked you *both* to come help us, then something must have happened. You must have—"

"What?" I demand. "I must have *what*?"

He looks to Mom, who gives her head a little shake. "Nothing," he says.

"No, tell me," I press. "What were you going to say? That I must have pissed her off? Made her leave?" I look at Mom. "It's always my fault somehow, right?"

She raises an eyebrow. "Well? Is it?"

"No!" I say. "All I wanted was to spend the day with her, and then she had to ruin it by being a selfish jerk, like it's *my* fault she lied to everyone about college. But it's not!"

"Hold on," Mom says. "*What* did she lie about?"

Oh god.

"Nothing," I say, shaking my head. "Never mind. It's not important."

I try to stand up, but Mom steps in front of the chair. "April, what did she lie about?"

"You should ask her."

"We're asking *you*," Dad says.

I squeeze my eyes shut. I want to take the words back so badly. As furious as I am with Jenn, I never meant to tell Mom and Dad her secret.

"April!"

I open my eyes. Mom and Dad are staring at me, their foreheads creased with worry, and it occurs to me that it's the first time they've looked at me like that in a long time. It figures it took talking about Jenn to make it happen.

"Please," Mom says. "Tell us what's going on."

"Jenn isn't going to community college in the fall," I say, defeated. "She's going to Stanford."

Mom sucks in a sharp breath. "That's not possible."

She turns to Dad, who's already on the phone. "She's not answering," he says. "Why isn't she answering?"

"I thought she was going home, but maybe she's still driving?"

Dads starts to pace the tiny office, and Mom sinks into the second desk chair. "I don't understand how this could happen," she says. "Are you *sure*?"

"She told me this morning."

"She has to answer her phone eventually," Dad says, still pacing, "and when she does, she is grounded."

Mom rolls her eyes. "She's eighteen, John. You can't ground her."

"Yes, I can!" Dad says. "As long as she lives under my roof, I can ground her."

"And when she sneaks out, then what?"

Dad scoffs. "Jenn wouldn't do that."

I glare at him. "So even though she *lied* to you, you're still acting like she's some kind of saint? I can't believe this."

"Not now, April," Mom snaps, cutting me off. "We don't need to ground her, John. There's still time to fix this."

Dad stops pacing. "Fix this? How are we going to *fix* this? She's already accepted!"

"I don't know!" Mom says. "I'm just saying we shouldn't panic—"

The front door opens, and two men walk in hand in hand. I expect Mom and Dad to stop arguing and go help them, but if anything their arguing gets louder.

"I know why she did this," Dad says. "It's because you pushed her to work so many hours in the store. She probably felt overwhelmed."

"So this is *my* fault?" Mom demands.

"Um," I say, "you guys?"

"That's not what I said," Dad says. "What I *said* is that if she hadn't been working so much, she might not have wanted to leave."

Up front, one of the customers leans in and whispers

something to the other. I can tell by the look on their faces that they're uncomfortable. My cheeks flush. This is so humiliating. "Dad, you should probably lower your voice—"

"I will not," Dad says. "Not until your mother admits that she's putting words in my mouth."

"But—"

"Hush, April," Mom says. "We don't need your input right now."

"But, *Mom*—"

"April!" Dad says. "For once, can you please just stay out of this?"

The customers turn around and leave. I sink back into my chair and watch Mom and Dad continue to battle. They're both standing now, their faces inches apart. Is this what it's like for Jenn every day? Running interference between our parents while strangers wander around the store, judging our dysfunctional family? No wonder she wanted to get away from here. *I* want to get away, and I've only been here for a little more than an hour.

I can't leave, though. Not yet. Not with my sister's angry words echoing in my head—*Poor April actually has to contribute for once.* I don't want her to be right. I don't want to be the selfish one. I want to make things better for my family, not worse. Especially after hearing what Mom told Aunt Harriet in the hall, about how sometimes she wishes she and Dad would split up. I can't let that happen. I won't.

"Excuse me," I say, standing. "Mom, Dad?" I wait for them to stop, but they keep arguing. I clear my throat and speak louder. "Do you guys still need someone to cover the store? Because I can . . . I *want* to help."

"What?" Dad says, turning to look at me. His face is surprised, like he forgot I was here entirely. "Oh, no. You can go home. We only needed Jenn anyway."

I flinch at his choice of words, but he doesn't notice. His attention is on Mom again. I grab my purse and head for the front door, not waiting for them to say goodbye.

My heart feels heavy in my chest as I walk the mile and a half home, like it's weighing me down to the ground. I want to talk to Jenn. I want to tell her I'm sorry, that I didn't realize things were so bad. But there's no chance she'll listen. And even if she did, I'm afraid of what else I might say. Because even though she has a right to be mad at me, the last hour has made it as clear as it's ever been that without her . . . our family doesn't stand a chance.

CHAPTER 20

JENN

Tom picks up his chopsticks and squeezes them in his right hand. The copper ring his dad got him for his seventeenth birthday shines in the dim restaurant lighting. "Thanks for coming early."

"Sure," I say.

My phone buzzes in my purse, and I switch it to silent. Mom and Dad keep calling me, probably trying to figure out why I'm not at the store, but I don't care. All my attention is on Tom, and making him tell me *why*—why he didn't return my calls all day, why he finally texted to ask if we could meet at four instead of six thirty, why he looks like he's about to break those chopsticks in half.

"I was glad to get out of the house again anyway," I say when it's clear no explanation is coming.

He rests the chopsticks on the little porcelain stand in front of him, then takes off his glasses and polishes them on the thick linen napkin. "Parents not taking it well?"

"I haven't told them yet," I say sheepishly.

Tom leans back in his seat.

"I'll do it soon, though! I promise. In fact, I'll do it right after we eat, when I get home."

He puts his glasses back on. "Good," he says, but his tone makes it clear he doesn't believe me.

"Actually, will you come with me? Please?"

Tom hesitates just long enough that I know I'm not going to like his answer. "I don't know," he says at last. "This is between you and your parents."

I nod like I understand, but I don't. Tom wanted me to tell them the truth weeks ago—months, really—but he knows how impossible they are. That's why I thought he'd say yes. I *needed* him to say yes.

The waiter approaches the table. "Welcome to Sakana Sushi," he says. "Have you been here before?"

"Yes," I say, smiling at Tom. "This is our favorite restaurant. Right?"

He nods again, but doesn't smile back. What is *wrong* with him?

"Great," the waiter says, "then you know everything is either prefix or Omakase—chef's choice. Can I get you something to drink?"

We each order an iced tea, and then he leaves. Normally Tom would start talking immediately—he can't stand those couples who sit at tables together, looking at their phones instead of talking to the people across from them—but instead we sit in silence while he fiddles with the soy sauce bottle.

"Have you finished packing?" I ask when the quiet becomes too much.

"This afternoon," he says. "My parents spent twenty minutes trying to convince me to bring the heavy rug from the attic for my dorm room. Then Peaches peed on it, and that pretty much put an end to the conversation."

"That cat is a menace."

He smiles. "Yeah. I'm going to miss her."

We settle back into silence. I unwrap my chopsticks and break them apart. I don't know what's going on between us, but I'm tired of tiptoeing around it. If there's something wrong, we need to talk about it.

"I missed you today," I say. "I tried texting and calling, but you didn't answer."

"Oh. I was packing and then spending some time with my parents, and I guess the day just got away from me." He clears his throat. "How was your day with April?"

"It started off nice. Then it deteriorated."

"What happened?"

"April happened. I told her about Stanford in the morning, and then she spent the rest of the day pouting. She also said some really mean things about my friends forgetting me when I move away, and then accused me of abandoning our family." I crumple the paper chopstick wrapper in my hand. "Can you believe that?"

Tom makes eye contact for what feels like the first time tonight. "Yeah, actually. I can."

I jerk back in my seat.

"I'm not saying she's right," he says quickly. "Especially the part about your friends. That's ridiculous. But I understand why she's angry with you."

I roll my eyes.

"I'm serious, Jenn. You kept this huge life change from her for a really long time, and she's probably upset that you didn't take her feelings into consideration." He clears his throat. "Like, you just expected her to support you, no questions asked. And, sure, that's what relationships are about sometimes, but people aren't only there to make you feel good, you know? You can't expect them to listen to your problems and call it a day. You have to give back."

"Are—are we still talking about April?"

Tom swallows, and shakes his head. "No. I don't think so."

The waiter comes to the table. An eternity passes as he pours iced tea from a decanter into each of our glasses, then places a small flower in mine. Normally, I love this part, but I just want him to go away.

"Are you ready to order?" he asks.

"Can we have a few more minutes to decide?" I ask.

The moment the waiter disappears, I lean forward. "Is that why you didn't return my texts and calls today? Because you're annoyed with me for not 'giving back'?"

"No," Tom says. "Well, yes, that's why. But I've also been thinking about things, and . . . I think we should talk."

"We *are* talking," I say, my voice rising. "So what is it? You think I'm not supportive of you? That I don't listen?"

Tom glances at the table to our right. A couple are

quietly sipping their green tea. There's no way they aren't hearing every word we say.

Tom lowers his voice. "I'm saying that we spend a lot of time talking about you and your family and how awful they are—"

"Oh, I'm *sorry*," I say. "I didn't realize you weren't interested in hearing about my life and my feelings. How silly of me."

"Don't do that," he says. "Don't put words in my mouth. You *know* I always want to hear how you're feeling. But sometimes it seems like all you want is an audience."

"That's not true. I ask for your opinion all the time—"

"But do you ever actually *listen?*" he says. "I told you months ago that you needed to tell your family the truth about moving, and you ignored me. In fact, I seem to remember you telling me I should *mind my own business.*" Tom laughs harshly. "Do you know how frustrating it is to be asked for help and then treated like you're being nosy?"

I pick up the small flower from my iced tea and fiddle with the petals. "I shouldn't have said that," I say. "It wasn't fair. Or true. I'm sorry. Really."

Tom sighs. "I know you are. But, Jenn, it happens all the time. You ask me for advice on dealing with your family, I give you my opinion, and then you ignore it and do the same thing you've always done—try to fix things for your parents instead of actually *communicating* what you're feeling. Then you come right back to me and it starts all over again, and nothing gets better—between them, or for you." He takes off his glasses and rubs his eyes, then puts them back on. "Sometimes I wonder if you really care all that much about them, or if you just like being the victim."

I drop the flower onto the table between us. "I cannot believe you just said that to me."

"I'm sorry," Tom says. "I shouldn't have. I'm just upset." He takes a sip of iced tea and clears his throat. "I guess what I'm really saying is that I'm tired of being caught in the middle. Do you understand?"

"Yeah . . . I do." I take a deep breath. "The good news is that we're about to move, so the problem is going away."

Tom shakes his head. "I don't think moving away is going to solve things, especially once they find out you've been lying. I think it's probably going to get worse."

"If you don't want to deal with me and my parents anymore, and you think things are going to get worse once we leave, then . . . what are you saying?"

Before he can answer, the waiter returns to the table. "We need another minute," Tom says. "Or . . . maybe five minutes?"

The waiter looks back and forth between us. Can he hear the blood rushing in my ears, feel my heart pounding in my chest?

"Of course," he says. "Take your time."

The waiter walks away, and Tom turns back to me.

"I'm not trying to hurt you," he says. "I'm really not. But we're starting a new chapter of our lives, and as much as I love you . . ." He looks down at his hands, and his eyes fill with tears. "I think maybe we should—"

My breath catches in my chest. "Oh my god. Are you breaking up with me?"

His face crumples. "I don't want to," he says. "I really don't."

This can't be happening. I won't let it. I reach across the table and grab his hand. "Then *don't*. Don't do it. We can work on this. We can fix it. *I* can fix it."

"There's nothing to fix, Jenn. It's just how you are—"

"Then I'll change!" I say. My hand starts to tremble in his. "Tom, *please*."

He squeezes my hand tightly. "You shouldn't have to change for anyone, Jenn. I just need space."

"You mean you need a break," I say. "No problem. For how long? A week? A month? We're going to be really busy when we first get to school, so it might be a good idea to focus on settling in. And then, once we do—"

"No," he says, releasing my hand. "No. I don't want to put a time limit on it."

"Okay, but—"

"And, actually, I don't want to call it a break, either, because then it feels like we're going to get back together no matter what."

"But . . . aren't we?"

"I don't know."

My eyes fill with tears. Of all the things I worried about today—April being upset, my parents freaking out—I never once imagined that Tom might not want to be with me anymore. Not when he didn't answer my calls, not when he didn't come to lunch. I never once thought the one person I could always turn to would leave me.

"When did you decide you didn't want to be with me anymore?" I ask, my voice raw.

Tom stares down at the table, like he's studying the grain in the wood. "I've been thinking about it for a while," he says, "but when I came over yesterday and you still hadn't told your parents the truth, I realized that I've been doing the same thing to you: withholding how I really feel. So when I got home, I made up my mind."

"Then why not just tell me last night on the phone? Why ignore me all day and then make me come to dinner if you were only going to dump me anyway?"

"I was going to say something last night, but then you told me about your sister's idea to spend the day together, and I thought maybe fixing things between the two of you would make this conversation easier."

"Easier on me?" I demand, glaring at him. "Or on *you?*"

The waiter comes back to the table. He must have noticed I'd stopped crying and figured, *Hey, this is a great time for raw fish, don't you think?*

"Are you ready to order?" he asks.

"No," Tom and I both say.

He smiles tightly. "Okay. I'll come back—"

"That's okay," I say, placing my napkin on the table. "I think we're going to be leaving instead."

"Uh . . . okay," the waiter says. "I'll get you a check."

When he's gone, I pull a five-dollar bill out of my wallet

and place it on the table. "That should cover the iced tea."

Tom nods. "Thanks."

I stand and straighten my clothes. I might have just been dumped, but that doesn't mean I'm going to walk out of here looking like it. But before I can walk away, Tom takes my hand. "I still love you, Jenn. You know that, right?"

My heart gives a little twist in my chest. "Bye, Tom."

Then I turn around and walk out of the restaurant as fast as I can, my eyes filling with tears again as I hurry toward the door. I wipe them away, refusing to let them fall. But the moment I shut myself inside my car, I let the tears win.

CHAPTER 21

APRIL

"I can't believe you told them about Stanford," Nate says as he kicks my soccer ball across the patch of grass behind his house. "Jenn's going to kill you when she gets home."

I've only been here for about thirty minutes—just long enough to have recovered from my long walk and to tell Nate everything—and already he's giving me a hard time.

"That's why I'm not going home." I block the ball with my bare foot and kick it back. "Ever."

Nate stops the ball but doesn't return it. "Oh . . . so you're staying here for a while, then?"

I frown. Nate's never asked me that before. We pretty much come and go as we please. "If that's okay?"

Nate shrugs and takes a few steps back. Then he runs toward the ball and kicks it—hard. I prepare myself to receive it, but the ball goes wide, spiraling into the avocado tree in the corner of his yard. A few avocados fall into the grass. His mom's going to kill him.

"I'll get it." I chase the ball down, but when I turn to kick it back, he's already sitting on the small porch attached to his house.

"What's up?" I ask, joining him.

He squints up into the sky. "Nothing."

"Not this again." I put the soccer ball on the ground and roll it back and forth with my foot. "Come on, what is it?"

He sighs. "It's Bo."

I stop messing with the ball. "Oh." Nate's older brother moved to Colorado for med school a few years ago, but dropped out when he realized he didn't want to be a doctor. "No luck finding a job, then?"

"He got one. He's gonna be a paralegal."

"Sounds fancy."

"Yeah," Nate says. "I guess."

We sit in silence for another few seconds, then I nudge him with my shoulder. "I feel like I'm missing something, but I don't know what it is. Do you *not* want him to be a paralegal?"

"No, it's a good job. That part's fine. But my mom's worried about him. At lunch, she said he almost never returns her calls." He looks down at his hands. "She thinks he's depressed."

The idea that Bo could be anything other than happy sends me for a loop. He's always joking around, and he's got a smile for everyone—just like Nate. But I know that doesn't mean anything. Cheerful people can still be depressed. "What do *you* think?" I ask. "Does Bo seem depressed to you?"

"I don't know," he says. "We haven't talked."

"Wait, what?" I turn on the steps so I'm facing him. "In how long?"

Nate grimaces. "Six months?"

"Six *months*? How can you go six months without talking to your own brother?"

Nate glares at me. "Let's see how often you and Jenn talk after *she* leaves."

His words hit me like a punch in the gut. "That was a little mean. You know things between us are rough."

Nate drops his head into his hands. "I'm sorry. I shouldn't have said that. I just feel bad enough already, you know? And what you said about not talking to him is exactly what my mom said right before she spent an hour guilt-tripping me about calling him once in a while."

"Is something going on between you guys? Jenn and I haven't been close in years, but you and Bo always seemed to get along really well."

Nate reaches down for the soccer ball and squeezes it between his hands. "We did get along. We still do, for the most part. It's just . . . I don't know how to talk to him about this, you know? What do you say to someone who's depressed?"

I chew on my lip. "Maybe it's not about saying anything specific. Just ask how they're doing."

"But what if he says things are really bad? What do I say

then?" He holds the ball to his chest. "What if he . . . cries?"

"Then he cries," I say gently. "You've seen me cry, and you handled it pretty well."

"That's different. You're my best friend."

"And he's your brother."

He sighs and puts his head between his knees. I want to comfort him, but I don't know what else to say. Not just because I'm not an expert on how to talk to someone with depression, but because he's right—Jenn and I barely talk as it is, and it's not likely things are going to get better once she leaves, especially not after how today turned out.

It's almost laughable how badly it went. If someone had told me yesterday, as I sorted through photos on the floor in the living room, that my perfect day—a day meant not only to cheer up my sister, but to reconnect with her—would result in us being further apart than ever, I probably wouldn't have even tried in the first place.

But that would mean I'd be right where Nate is now, head between my knees, wanting to help but not knowing how.

I bump my knee against his. "It's not too late, you know. You can still call him. We can do it together, if you want."

Nate sits up. "Really? You'd do that?"

"Sure," I say. "I'd do anything for you."

I blush as soon as the words leave my mouth. What am I *doing*, talking to Nate like that? But he just smiles. "Maybe later, okay?"

I shrug, relieved that he's not going to give me a hard time. "Sure."

"So what are we going to do the rest of the night?" he asks, standing. "Do you want to watch a movie or something?"

I turn around on the porch steps and look inside Nate's house. The living room is cozy and inviting, and the allure of snuggling into my usual spot on the right side of his couch while we watch Netflix is strong. But we've done that at least three times a week since summer started, and with school right around the corner, it feels like we should do something else. Something bigger.

Plus, if I don't keep myself busy, the likelihood that I text that asshole Eric is a whole lot higher.

I turn back to Nate. "Jenn and I didn't finish the list. Would you want to do the rest with me?"

Nate clutches his chest. "You're inviting me to your *Special Sister Day?*"

I groan. "I hate you so much."

He laughs, and this time his smile is full-blown. "I'm in. What's left to do?"

"Let me look at the list." I reach into my pocket, but my phone isn't there. "Hold on a sec."

I cross Nate's backyard and grab my purse out of the grass. I root around inside, but come up empty-handed.

"What are you looking for?" Nate asks.

"My phone." I dump the contents. Chapstick, two tampons, a receipt from lunch, sunglasses, a compact, earbuds, and my house keys tumble out . . . but no phone. "Oh, no. I think I forgot it at the store."

"We can go get it."

I look across the yard to my house. The lights are all off, which means Mom and Dad are probably still at the store. I could go grab it. But after the way my last visit went, I'm in no hurry to go back. "Let's get it later tonight. There were only four stops left on the list anyway. And we can make up our own stuff too."

"What if someone texts you?" Nate asks.

I start shoving everything back into my purse. "I'll just talk to them later."

"But won't Eric worry?"

My fingers freeze around my house keys. "Um, no. I don't think he will."

I don't want to tell Nate about the text. The whole thing is humiliating, and every time I think about it, a flush of embarrassment races across my skin and my stomach cramps up.

"Suit yourself," Nate says. He picks up my boots from the grass and tosses them to me. "Let's go."

CHAPTER 22

JENN

The drive home is a miserable blur. I follow every traffic signal, obey every law. I even smile when Mrs. Iniguez from down the block waves at me as I drive past her house. But inside, in the place I never let anyone see, I am screaming at the top of my lungs.

The house is empty. On any other day I'd take advantage of this by reading in bed, or stretching out on my yoga mat and daydreaming about all the things Tom and I are going to do next year—the classes we'll take, the people we'll meet, how happy we'll be once we're finally away from home.

But none of that's going to happen now, and the only thing louder than the suffocating silence is the awful realization playing on an endless loop in my mind—*I was wrong about Tom*. So instead, I let the scream in my head *out*. I scream and scream until my throat burns and my face is wet from crying. Then I collapse onto my bed.

How could I have let this happen?

I try to bury my face in my bed, but the quilt Grandma gave me scratches my face, so I turn my head to the side, but then I catch the scent of mothballs and immediately start coughing. I hate this stupid quilt, but I can't get rid of it, no matter how many times April always makes fun of me for keeping it. *It's so old and itchy. Grandma isn't going to find out if you throw it away.* But things like that are easy for April. She doesn't waste time worrying or overthinking. She just does whatever she wants.

Easy to do when other people's feelings don't matter to you, I guess.

My phone rings, and I sit up so fast it makes me light-headed. I search the bed, but I can't find it anywhere. It rings again. *Crap.* What if it's Tom, calling to tell me it was all a mistake? I can't let it go to voicemail. He might change his mind—

It rings again, and I realize the phone is on my desk. I lunge for it, swiping to answer before I've even read the screen. "Tom?"

"Hello! This is an automatic call from—"

I end the call and shove my phone back into my purse. I can't stay here. I have to do something to beat back the grief and rage twisting inside me before it makes me crazy. Plus, Mom and Dad could come home from work any minute, and I am *not* ready to talk to them about Stanford. Or anything else, for that matter.

I grab my phone and purse and head back out to the car.

• • •

Shruthi lives at the end of a cul-de-sac just outside downtown Culver City. Like all the houses on her street, Shruthi's is big and white and sits at the end of a driveway lined with colorful flowers. I ring the doorknob and step back, my hands clasped in front of me. As always, I'm rewarded with the sound of frantic barking and toenails scrambling across hardwood—the signal that Pancake is on her way.

"Down!" Shruthi says on the other side of the door. "Get *down*, Pancake. What is wrong with you?"

There's a scuffle, and then the door opens. Shruthi appears, one hand on the door, the other holding her giant golden retriever back by the collar. "Oh, it's you!" she says. "No wonder she's freaking out."

She lets go of Pancake, who immediately jumps all over me. I drop to my knees and hug her furry, wiggly body . . . and burst into tears.

"Oh my gosh," Shruthi says, kneeling beside me to rest a hand on my back. "Are you okay? What happened?"

"I'm—so—sorry," I choke out, my arms still wrapped around the dog. "I didn't mean—to—cry—"

"No one ever *means* to cry," Shruthi says, rubbing my back. "It's okay. Let it out."

I sniffle and wipe my eyes, then let Pancake go. She licks my face and runs back into the house, her duty as Welcome Dog complete.

Shruthi helps me to my feet. "Do you want to come in? We're cooking—"

"Oh, I'm so sorry," I say, backing away. "I'll go."

"No!" Shuthi says, pulling me inside. "I was just saying that if you come in, my amma will make you help. It's the family rule—if you're eating, you're helping."

I'm about to tell her I don't need to eat, I'll be fine, when the smell of garlic and onion reaches me. My stomach grumbles. "Are you sure it's okay if I stay?"

"Totally," Shruthi says. "Amma! Jenn is staying for dinner."

"Good," Mrs. Thakur calls from the kitchen. "She can help cook."

Shruthi smirks. "Told you."

We go into the brightly lit kitchen. Mrs. Thakur is standing at the sink, rinsing what looks like ten to twenty whole chickens. The counters are covered in vegetables, pots of rice soaking in water, tubs of plain yogurt, and small bowls of brightly colored spices. Two steel pots bubble on the stove, their contents covered by heavy lids. "Wow," I say. "This is a lot of food."

"It's not for tonight," Mrs. Thakur says, waving hello to me with a wet hand. "Amara is turning seven tomorrow, so we're having a party."

"More like a festival," Shruthi mumbles beside me. "She's inviting her entire class, plus their parents."

"*And* my ballet class," Amara says, appearing in the doorway. "Miss Yasmin said they're going to perform a special dance for me."

Mrs. Thakur holds out one arm, and Amara rushes forward and buries her face in her mother's side. Shruthi rolls her eyes.

"You girls go pick the leaves off the coriander," Mrs. Thakur says, pointing to Shruthi and me. "I'm making dhania chicken for tomorrow."

"It's my favorite," Amara says.

"It's *my* favorite," Shruthi corrects. "Not yours. And it's also a total pain to make. Amma, can't you make something else? It'll take forever to prep enough coriander for this many chickens."

"When it's *your* birthday, *you* can choose what to make for dinner," Mrs. Thakur says. "Get to work."

Amara sticks out her tongue at her sister, then hides her face in Mrs. Thakur's robes again. Shruthi sighs and pulls two produce bags from the fridge. "This will get us started."

Shruthi grabs two plates and leads me out of the kitchen to the dining room. We sit down next to each other at the table, and Shruthi dumps the contents of a bag onto a plate.

"Oh," I say, picking up a thin, leafy stem. "Are coriander and cilantro the same thing?"

"Yup," Shruthi says.

"Cool. I love cilantro."

"Prepare to hate it by the time we're finished. This is going to take forever."

We get to work pulling the leaves off the stems and piling them on the plates. Shruthi is right—it takes a long time to get through the bags—but I don't mind. My mind feels blissfully quiet for the first time since I left the restaurant. I don't think about Tom, or my parents, or anything really. I just focus on plucking the little green leaves, one at a time.

The distraction doesn't last.

"So," Shruthi says when we're halfway through the bag. "Do you want to talk about what happened?"

I shake my head.

"Okay," she says. "You don't have to."

She twists a discarded coriander stem around her finger. Then she lets go, and it springs back. She picks it up again and twists it around her finger a second time. I watch her do this, over and over again. When it springs back for the fifth time, I exhale, and look up at her face.

"Tom broke up with me," I say. "He said I don't listen to him. He wants to take a break."

Shruthi twists the stem around her finger again. "A break?"

"Yes," I say. "Actually . . . no. He said he didn't want to call it that. He also didn't want to put a time limit on it."

"Hmm."

"And now I'm not sure what I'm going to do." I pick up a coriander stem and wind it around my finger, just like Shruthi did. Instead of letting it go, I twist it even tighter. "Maybe April's right. Maybe I should defer a year."

"April said that?" Shruthi asks.

"She wasn't talking about Tom when she said it, but she's still right—I can't go to Stanford without him, Shruthi. We had everything planned out. We're even in the same dorm. If I run into him . . . I just can't do it."

Shruthi crosses her arms and fixes me with a stare so similar to the one her mom gave her in the kitchen that it makes me sit up straighter in my chair.

"I know what you're thinking, okay? I need to call him and talk it through."

"No," Shruthi says.

"No?"

"No. I think he made what he wants pretty clear." My eyes fill with tears again, but she keeps talking. "What's *not* clear is what *you* want."

I wipe my eyes with the back of my hand. "I want Tom. I want to be with him."

"Okay," she says. "But what else? You want more out of life than just dating Tom, right?"

"Of *course*," I say, bristling. "Of course I do."

"Good. Like what?"

I look down at my hands and rub the little red line left behind on my index finger by the coriander stem. "I wanted to go to Stanford, but now—"

"Why?" she asks, cutting me off. "Why did you want to go to Stanford?"

I sit back in the dining room chair. "Um . . . because it's a really good school? They have a well-respected biomedical science program."

She frowns. "I didn't know you were interested in that."

"Oh, I'm not, but Tom—"

"—is interested in biomed," Shruthi says, nodding. "Which is why he applied there. But do you remember why *you* applied?"

I swallow, and tears fill my eyes. "I just wanted to be with him."

"No!" Shruthi says, and slaps the table.

I jump in my seat.

"Jenn, listen to me," Shruthi says, leaning forward. "You've been talking about Stanford for as long as I've known you, and you had a reason for wanting to go there *way* before you met Tom."

I sniff and wipe my eyes. "I don't remember."

Shruthi fixes me with her mother's stare again. "You said you wanted to go there because it's the best of all worlds— great science facilities, amazing arts departments, you name it. You said Stanford would give you a 'world-class liberal arts education.' We were only in tenth grade and you were already thinking like a college counselor." Shruthi shakes her head. "But it wasn't just that. You also said you wanted to be closer to your grandma. Doesn't she live up there?"

"Yeah, in San Mateo," I say.

"Has any of that changed?"

I shake my head.

Shruthi sits back in her chair, a look of satisfaction on her face. "Then you should still go," she says. "Regardless of whether you're dating Tom."

"I don't hear you picking coriander!" Mrs. Thakur calls from the kitchen. "Shruthi, come get another bag. You still have fifteen to go!"

Shruthi grimaces. "Be right back."

She goes into the kitchen, leaving me alone in the dining room with the pile of coriander leaves and discarded stems. I pick one up, but this time I pop one of the bright green leaves into my mouth instead of winding the stem around my finger. Shruthi's right. I know she is. But the idea of walking onto that huge campus without Tom still terrifies me. For the last year I've pictured us doing everything together—classes, meals, Friday nights—but now that I know he won't be there, I can't see myself there either. It's as if by erasing *us*, he's erased me, too.

"Sorry about that," Shruthi says as she comes back into the room. She dumps a second bag of coriander on the table. "Mom says if we finish this one, then she'll heat up some leftovers from last night. I know that doesn't sound very appetizing, but curry is actually better the next day."

"I've had some of your lunch at school," I say. "I trust anything that comes out of your mom's kitchen."

"I made it this time, actually," she says. "But she taught me."

I grin. "Even better."

Shruthi picks up a piece of coriander and gets back to work. I feel a little better now that I've told her about Tom, but now that that's out of the way, I notice the way she's sitting—her legs tightly crossed, her lips pursed—is strange.

So is the way she's ripping the leaves off the stems.

"Is everything okay?" I ask. "I mean, between you and me?"

"Sure."

She keeps tearing the leaves away from the stems, one after another.

"Shruthi," I say.

"Hmm?"

"Look at me, please?"

She hesitates, then puts the coriander down. "What's up?"

"I'm sorry about today," I say. "I was a jerk at lunch."

"Yes," she says, nodding. "You were. What I don't get is *why*."

I'm on the verge of telling her the truth, when I realize . . . I don't want to tell her what my sister said. Not just because I'm embarrassed that I was so easily manipulated—though I *am*—but because a teeny, tiny part of me isn't sure April was wrong. I didn't invent them leaving me out of their conversation about UCLA, nor did I imagine the way they leaned in to talk to each other the moment I stepped away from the table.

But I don't want to tell Shruthi that because it'll just start an argument, and the last thing I want to do right now is get into a fight in the middle of her dining room with Mrs. Thakur only a few feet away. So I bottle it up instead and say, "I was in a bad mood, I guess."

Shruthi considers me for a moment, then picks up another stem. "If you don't keep working, we're never going to eat."

"Sorry," I say, returning to the pile of greens. I clear my throat. "I'd rather pick coriander all night than go home, though."

"Why?"

"Because when I get home," I say, "I have to tell my parents about Stanford."

"What about it?"

"That I'm going. They, um . . . still think I'm staying here."

Shruthi drops the coriander she's picking. "I thought you told them weeks ago!" She shakes her head. "This isn't right."

"I know," I say, struggling to keep my tone even. First April and Tom, now Shruthi. "I was hoping Tom was going to help me tell them tonight—"

"Tonight is *now*," Shruthi says. "It's already almost seven!"

She bags the rest of the coriander and stands. "Come on. I'm getting you some dinner, and then we're going."

"Wait, you're coming with me? You don't have to do that."

"I know," she says, "but if you haven't noticed, I'm a really, *really* good friend."

CHAPTER 23

APRIL

O ur first stop is Van Leeuwen in Culver City. Technically it was supposed to be the *last* stop, but after the day I've had, ice cream is a priority.

We both order the usual—salted caramel for me, honeycomb for him—and grab a table on the empty patio out back. It makes me a little sad to be here without Jenn, but the ice cream helps.

"Whoa," Nate says as I eat three sweet-and-salty bites in quick succession.

"What? It's delicious." I reach across the table and swipe a bite of his with my spoon. "Why do I always forget that honeycomb is better?"

The door opens, and two girls on a date come outside. One of them winks at me as they sit down at the table next to ours. It takes me a minute to figure out why, and then I realize—she thinks Nate and I are on a date too. I shake my head, but she's already turned away.

"So, what's left to do on the list?" Nate asks when we've finished our ice cream. "Anything particularly good?"

I glance at my purse. On the way over, I remembered the envelope of photos is still inside, so technically I don't need the list on my phone. But I don't tell Nate that. He'd want to see the pictures, and I'm not sure I want to look at Jenn's face right now, regardless of the fact that she's no older than fourteen in most of them. "We were going to head toward Beverly Hills and do a few things over on that side of town, and then the last stop was coming here for ice cream."

"Cheers," Nate says, lifting his spoon.

I take another bite, and my thoughts return to the envelope. Our parents printed most of the photos for a photo album that never actually came together. But there's one photo that *isn't* in the envelope, because my parents have never seen it. No one has, because it's been sitting in my cell phone since the day I took it.

It was a few weeks into Jenn's freshman year, and we'd just spent the entire summer hanging out at the ice rink and playing Crazy Eights on the roof of our duplex while the sun set. Then she started high school, and for the first time we weren't at the same school anymore. No more walking together in the morning or running into each other in the halls as she hurried to eighth-grade PE and I stalled before sixth-grade science. We had to wait until we got home to talk.

That's why we decided to go to Van Leeuwen that day — to catch up. Jenn hadn't made many friends yet, and I was already struggling in history even though we were only a few weeks into the semester. We were halfway through eating our ice cream when I noticed Jenn checking out a guy in line. I asked if she knew him from high school, but she blushed and changed the subject. Then, when she went to the bathroom, I noticed *him* noticing *her*. So when Jenn came back from the bathroom, I offered him a seat at our table . . . then conveniently realized I had to make a phone call the moment he sat down.

As soon as I got inside, I turned around and snapped the very first picture of them ever taken—the picture on my cell phone.

I wasn't sure about including Van Leeuwen in today's itinerary. I'm not in that photo, so technically it's not about Jenn and me. But I wanted Jenn to remember that, even though it's a picture of her and Thomas, I was there too. I was there *first*. And if I hadn't been, not only would the picture not exist, *Jenn and Thomas* might not either.

But after what she said in the car—about how I made everything about *me* instead of *us*—it's probably for the best that she didn't see it. She'd say I was being selfish again, and worse, she'd probably be right.

The door opens again, and another couple comes outside and sits on the other side of the patio.

"We should go," Nate says suddenly.

"Why?" I ask. "We just got here. I haven't even finished eating—"

"I know," he says, standing. "But we should get you some real dinner. Ice cream isn't good for you."

"I think I'll be okay, *Mom*. Will you please sit back down?" I glance over at the two girls seated a few feet away. "People are going to think we're in a fight or something."

"No," Nate says, his eyes widening as he stares at something over my shoulder. "Let's go."

"What the hell is wrong is with you?" I ask, turning around. "What are you looking at— *Oh.*"

Ten feet away from us, seated at a table in the corner of the patio, is Eric, his hands tangled in the curly brown hair of the girl he's with. The girl he's *kissing*.

"Come on," Nate says. "You don't have to watch this."

But I'm not listening to him. I'm too busy touching my own curls, remembering the way Eric's hands felt in my hair when he kissed me just a few hours ago. "Mother. Fucker."

Nate's eyes go wide. "Shh, they're going to hear you."

Shit. I did not mean to say that out loud.

The brunette breaks away from Eric and looks over. "April?"

Oh god. It's Blair, from my trig class. I raise a hand and smile weakly. "Hey."

"Hi! How's your summer going?" Blair smiles, and I notice her lipstick is a little smudged from kissing. My stomach churns. I should *not* have eaten that ice cream so fast.

"Oh, sorry," Blair says, reaching out for Eric's hand. "This is Eric. Or do you guys already know each other?"

Eric stares daggers at me, but his voice is light and friendly. "A little, yeah. April and I both play soccer."

"Oh, right," Blair says. "Of course."

Eric continues to stare me down, even as he places his hand on Blair's. My heart squeezes in my chest. I know what he's doing. He's making it clear that I am not supposed to let on that we're dating. Correction—that we *were* dating. If that's what we were even doing. Oh god, what *were* we doing? And what are *they* doing? Is she his girlfriend now? He never took me out for ice cream. He never took me *anywhere*. We always just met up somewhere private, like my room, or his car.

I guess that's the difference between what he does when he really likes someone and what he does when he just wants to have sex.

My eyes start to burn, and I know I'm thirty seconds away from crying. I start to turn away and realize Nate is watching me. "Are you okay?" he asks.

I shake my head.

"Okay," he says. "Let's go."

We start for the exit. Behind us, Blair calls, "See you around, April!"

I hesitate, my hand on the door. I have to say something. I don't want to be rude to her—she didn't do anything wrong. But I know the minute I open my mouth, I'll start to cry.

Nate puts his hand on my back. "I've got this."

He turns around and strides toward their table. "Hi, I'm Nate," he says to Blair, extending his hand.

"Nice to meet you," she says, a look of surprise on her face as they shake hands.

"You too. We're going to get out of your way, but I thought you might want to know one thing before we go."

Blaire blinks. "Um, okay?"

"This guy you're with?" Nate says, gesturing to Eric. "He's a piece of shit."

Then he turns around, grabs my hand, and pulls me outside.

CHAPTER 24

JENN

re you ready?" Shruthi asks.

We've been sitting in the car for almost ten minutes, staring at my duplex. The white stucco walls are bright against the darkening summer sky, and inside, the chandelier my parents found twenty years ago on their honeymoon in Italy casts a warm, welcoming glow. Mom is seated on the couch, while Dad walks back and forth past the front window. It would be the picture of comfort and happiness . . . if they weren't screaming at each other.

"Don't be nervous," Shruthi says. "I'm sure they'll understand once you explain."

"I doubt it," I say.

My dad throws his hands up in the air, and Shruthi winces. "I'll admit, your dad looks kinda . . ."

"Pissed?" I say. She nods.

Mom stands, and begins rearranging pillows on the couch, something she does when she's so furious she can't sit still. It usually means I have about five minutes to calm things down before she totally loses it.

Normally, I'd hurry inside to interrupt whatever they're fighting about and save them from themselves. It would be the right thing to do. But today isn't a normal day, so I stay put.

Shruthi clears her throat. "Do you have a plan?"

I shake my head. A plan would have been a good idea — we've been sitting here long enough that I probably could have come up with one — but every time I try to imagine myself telling my parents the truth, my mind goes back to Tom. Or, more specifically, the look on his face when he told me he wanted to break up. He seemed sad, but also scared. Was he afraid he was going to regret breaking up with me? Or that he might not have the courage to go through with it? And then, when I was leaving, he said he loved me . . . but he also said he wasn't sure he ever wanted to get back together. How can both those things be true at the same time?

I reach for my phone. I put it on silent at dinner, and I haven't checked it since. The screen is full of missed calls and unread texts from Mom and Dad, but nothing from Tom. My heart sinks.

"Jenn?" Shruthi says. "I think they see us."

I look up. Mom and Dad are standing in the doorway to the house, staring at the car.

"Crap. I better go in."

"Want me to go with you?"

"I think I'd better do this on my own." I hand Shruthi the

keys. "Wanna drive yourself home? I'll bike over when we're done and pick up the car."

Shruthi nods. "Good luck."

I climb out and walk slowly across the street. Mom's arms are crossed, and Dad looks like he might start yelling again at any moment. It occurs to me that they might not just be mad at each other—they might be mad at *me* for not showing up at the store too. I take a deep breath and speed up. Might as well get this over with.

"Hi," I say when I'm a few feet away from the front door. "Sorry I didn't come earlier—"

"When were you going to tell us?" Mom interrupts. "Or were you going to keep lying forever?"

I come to an abrupt stop. "What?"

"Don't play dumb," she says. "April told us everything."

My stomach sinks. Of course she did. *Of course.* I bet she couldn't wait to rat me out after our fight in the car.

"Well?" Dad says. "We're waiting."

I glance over my shoulder. Shruthi is still in the passenger seat, her face ghost white as she watches us. This is *not* how I wanted to tell them. "Can we go inside?" I ask.

I scurry past them into the house, not waiting for an answer. Mom and Dad follow me, slamming the door behind us.

Dad stands in the middle of the living room. "Sit down."

I drop onto the couch and fold my hands in my lap. Mom and Dad stand in front of me, their faces matching masks of fury. I swallow and examine my fingers. I've never been in any real trouble before, at least not like this. But I've seen Mom and Dad argue a million times. I can handle this.

"I know you're upset," I say carefully.

"You're damn right," Dad says.

"But I think if you sit down," I continue, gesturing to the empty seats beside me, "I can explain everything. What's important to keep in mind is—"

Mom holds up a hand. "Jennifer, don't talk to us like we're children. In fact, you are not to speak unless we ask you a direct question. Do you understand?"

I almost choke on my surprise. They've never spoken to me like this before. To April? Yes. But to me? Never. "Mom, the thing is—"

"*Do you understand?*" she repeats.

I nod and sink back into the couch. This is already not going well.

"We have been calling you for hours," she says. "We have left text messages. We even called Tom's parents. Do you have any idea how worried we were?"

My cheeks flush. They probably told the Alberts everything—not just that I wasn't answering my phone, but about college, too.

I bet Tom's parents are relieved he dumped me. Who wants their son dating a liar?

"Explain yourself," Dad says. "Explain all of this. Right now."

I look back and forth between them. I've been picturing this moment for months—I knew I'd have to tell them the truth, and then somehow find a way to ask them to cover the rest of my college expenses—but I never once actually planned what I was going to *say*. "I'm not sure where to start."

Mom glares at me. "How about you start with deciding to go to a college we agreed you weren't attending? Or maybe with how you forced your grandmother to lie on your behalf and pay the down payment?"

I wince at the mention of Grandma. She must be so disappointed in me.

"Well?" Dad prompts.

"Technically," I say, struggling to keep my voice calm, "I didn't agree to anything. You and Dad talked privately, then *informed* me that I wasn't going to Stanford. And for the record," I continue, my voice growing stronger, "I didn't force Grandma. She thought I should go too."

"But *why*?" Dad asks. "There are plenty of good schools here. I don't understand what it is about Stanford that's so important to you."

I take a long, slow breath. I can practically hear Tom's voice in my head, urging me to tell the truth—that I need to get away from their fighting, from the store. From *them*. That living in this house hurts me. But it'll just make this situation worse.

"I don't get it," Dad says. "You're usually such a good kid."

"*Usually?*" I say, my temper flaring. "I'm always a good kid, Dad. In fact, I'm a *great* kid."

"A great kid wouldn't do this," Mom says. "A great kid wouldn't put us in this position."

"What position?" I demand. "I got into Stanford. You should be proud of me!"

"We *are* proud," Mom says. "That isn't even a question. But you know we need you at the store."

"You could hire someone—"

"We can't afford to do that," Mom snaps, "not with sales the way they are." She takes a deep breath, then sits next to me on the couch and takes my hands in hers. "Listen. We know college is important to you. We really do. But we need you here. At least for now."

I try to pull my hand away, but she holds firm.

"We know you'll have to cut back on your hours now that you're going to community college. That's why we plan to ask your sister to pick up a little of the slack."

"A few hours isn't going to make a difference," I say through gritted teeth. "What I need is—"

"Let's not get ahead of ourselves," Dad says, holding up a hand. "I understand you'd like to cut back more than that, but you know how April is. She's too disorganized to be trusted with the store for more than a few hours. She'd probably get distracted and forget about the customers."

I'm still upset with April, but it irks me to hear them say that about her, especially since that's exactly what *they* do at the store—get distracted by their endless fights and forget what they're supposed to be doing.

"That's not really fair," I say. "She's not *that* unorganized. She put together an entire itinerary for us today, and it went almost perfectly."

"That was very nice of her," Dad says. "But even if she's up to the challenge, she can't handle taking over *all* your shifts. She can't come in until almost three, when school's over."

"Actually, she can't come in then, either. She has soccer practice."

Mom gives Dad a *look*, then turns back to me. "April's going to have to miss some practice, then, because we're short staffed even with you and Nate working in the store. She won't like it at first, but eventually she'll understand."

She'll understand. I remember April's face in the boat when I told her the same thing. At the time, I thought she was being immature. But hearing Mom say it now, like April's life and her interests are so obviously second to what she and Dad want that it's barely even worth discussing? I suddenly understand *exactly* why she was so angry with me in the car.

"No," I say. "She won't understand, and her team won't either. You can't do that to her. You can't make her give it up."

Dad throws his hands up. "Then that leaves us back where we started, Jenn. We need your help at the store. It's the only way to keep it open." He takes a seat in a chair by the window and clasps his hands together. I've seen him sit like this a million times when he worked at the bank. It never boded well for the other guy. "I'm sorry," he says, "but there's nothing else to be done. We need you here."

I look back and forth between my parents. "So that's

it? You're not going to let me go? We've barely even talked about it!"

Mom squeezes my hand. "Honey, you were never supposed to go in the first place."

"But—but I *have* to go. I've worked so hard for this." I turn to face Mom on the couch. "I'm supposed to get on a plane tomorrow morning!"

She shakes her head, and my heart plummets into my stomach.

"Fine," I say, standing. "Fine. I didn't want to do this, but you're not giving me any choice." I smooth my clothes, and take a deep breath. Here goes nothing. "I'm eighteen years old, which means I'm an adult. It *also* means I don't actually *need* your permission. I'm going to Stanford tomorrow, and there's nothing you can do about it."

Dad leans back in his chair and crosses his arms. "You're right. We can't stop you. But that doesn't mean we have to *help* you either, and if what your grandma tells me is correct, you can't afford to go on your own. You need help covering room and board, among other things."

I sink back down onto the couch. "I can't believe this," I say.

Mom reaches for my hand. "You've worked hard," Mom says. "We know that. And we want you to get a good education at a good school. But we need you to stay in LA, at least for now."

The numb realization that I've failed slowly dawns on me. For the last six months, I've tried to imagine every possible snag in my plan, every tiny little road bump I might encounter along the way. I planned everything so perfectly, from which schools Tom and I applied to, to how I'd intercept my admissions packet when it came in the mail, to how I'd pack my clothes in the days leading up to the move without my parents noticing I was doing it.

The only thing I never prepared for was the one thing I should have seen coming: that in the end, my parents would do what they always do.

They'd put themselves first.

CHAPTER 25

APRIL

"Where to?" Nate asks the second we're back in the car. He's gripping the steering wheel so hard you'd think he was navigating a twisting mountain road, not sitting motionless in the parking lot. "The beach? Or maybe Johnnie's Pastrami? We can go wherever you want." He hits the steering wheel. "Actually, let's go to his house. We'll wait till he gets home, and then beat the shit out of him."

I slide down in my seat, and cover my face with my hands. I can't believe this. Of all the places in LA we could have gone . . .

"I'm sorry," Nate says. "It's just, you guys are dating! What the hell is he doing out with another girl?"

"We're not," I say.

"Not what?"

I drop my hands. "Dating. We're not dating. He's not my

boyfriend, and I'm not his girlfriend, so technically he didn't do anything wrong."

"*Bullshit*," Nate says, so viciously that I flinch. "You were seeing each other exclusively, right?"

"I thought so. But he never actually *said* that—"

"It doesn't matter! He was having sex with you and didn't tell you he was *also* having sex with other people. Right?"

I blush and look away. Nate and I talk about who's hooking up with who at school, but we've never talked about who *we're* sleeping with before. Like when he was seeing Rachel from band at the beginning of last year—I knew they were hanging out, but I never asked him what *else* they were doing. Partly because I didn't want to know, and partly because it made me irrationally angry to picture him hooking up with someone who so *clearly* wasn't right for him.

"Right," I say. "But I probably should have just assumed he was screwing around. Everyone wants to hook up with him."

"That's beside the point," Nate says. "If you're having sex with multiple people, they should know." He cracks his knuckles and mumbles, "You deserve better than that. Better than *him*."

My stomach does a little somersault, and through the haze of my sadness, I find myself wanting to ask him if he has someone specific in mind. But that's the kind of flirtatious thing I'd say to *Eric*, not Nate.

I shake the thought from my head. "Let's just drop this, okay?"

"Are you sure? I wasn't serious about beating him up,

but we could TP his house like in those old movies my dad watches."

A smile pulls at the corner of my mouth, but I shake my head. "I just want to forget he exists, at least for a few hours. Okay?"

"Done," Nate says. "So what do you want to do instead? What was next on your itinerary?"

I try to picture the list in my head. "I think Rodeo Drive was up next. We were going to do some window-shopping and make fun of all the tourists ogling overpriced handbags or whatever."

Nate makes a noise in the back of his throat.

"Oh, come on," I say, "it's not like we were actually going to *say* anything to them—"

"It's not that," he says. "It's just, it doesn't really sound like something Jenn would want to do. I mean, I know she's picky about what she wears, but she doesn't really strike me as the window-shopping type. That's more a *you* thing."

I groan. "You sound just like her."

"I highly doubt that," Nate says. He starts the car but doesn't make any moves to actually leave the parking lot.

"You totally do. When we got into a fight earlier, Jenn said today was all about stuff *I* wanted to do. Then she called me selfish."

Nate frowns. "That's a little harsh. I mean, Rodeo Drive doesn't sound like a winner, but I'm sure there were tons of stops on that list that were perfect for her. Didn't you go to the Ferris wheel? Everyone likes that."

"That's what I thought." I turn in my seat a little so I'm facing him. "Did you know that it's possible to throw up all over your big sister and then completely forget it ever happened?"

He stares at me, horrified. "Are you serious?"

I nod.

"You *didn't.*"

"Trust me," I say. "I did."

Nate bursts out laughing. "Oh my god. I wish I could have seen her face." He mimes staring down in horror at a puke-stained shirt, and cracks up again.

I swat at him, but now I'm laughing too. "You're making me feel even worse!"

"Okay, okay," he says, though I can tell he's struggling not to keep laughing. "You're right. You probably could have picked something better to start the day off."

"The thing is, even if I could redo the whole day, I don't know where we should have gone instead." I sink back in my seat. "Thank god she doesn't actually want to meet up tonight. There's no way I could come up with something meaningful to both of us in the next hour if I couldn't do it yesterday, when I had all day to plan."

Nate looks at me funny. "Wait—meet up? What are you talking about?"

"You know, what I said at the end of our fight about meeting at eight."

"Uh, no," Nate says. "I have no clue what you're talking about."

"Oh," I say. "I guess I forgot to tell you." I kick my boots off, and put my feet up on the dashboard. Might as well get comfortable if we're not going anywhere. "We were fighting, and Jenn said if I really cared about her I would've taken her to a place that's important to *both* of us, not just me. Then I said, *I'll meet you there at eight o'clock.* Then she drove away."

"That's it?" Nate asks. "That's how the fight ended?"

"Yep." I reach for the radio. The oldies station Nate's mom insists he keeps programmed blares out of the speakers. I change the channel. "It was stupid, obviously. We're not actually doing it."

I start to sing along to the radio, but Nate turns the volume down. "Hold on . . . Are you sure Jenn knows you aren't meeting?"

"She must. We didn't pick a place, and we haven't talked since she left me in front of the store."

"But it's possible, right? That she took you seriously, and thinks you're meeting"—he checks the clock—"in just over an hour?"

The truth of the situation hits me with a jolt. He's right—I have no way of knowing if Jenn took me seriously or not. I mean, she probably didn't—she never does—but if she *did* and she shows up at this mystery location and I'm not there? I can't let her down like that. Especially when this was my ridiculous idea in the first place.

"Can I borrow your phone?" I ask Nate.

He pulls his cell out of his pocket but doesn't hand it to me. "Maybe you shouldn't."

"Of course I should," I say, reaching for the phone. "I

need to make sure she knows we aren't actually meeting. Otherwise, she's gonna show up and I'll look like a total flake."

"I know," he says. "But hear me out. She's about to move away—"

"*Maybe*," I say. "You didn't see how pissed our parents were."

"Which means you only have one more night living together in the same place." He puts the phone face down on the dashboard. "What if this is your only chance to make things right with your sister before she moves away? If you call it off, you're forfeiting the opportunity."

I look down at my lap. After what he told me about his brother and him not talking, I totally get why he'd want me to talk to Jenn before things get any worse. But it doesn't make this easier.

"For the sake of argument," I say, "let's say I meet up with her tonight. What would I tell her? *Sorry I took you to a bunch of places that were apparently traumatic for you as a child, then tried to manipulate you into staying in LA. I didn't know Mom and Dad were such assholes to you—please forgive me?*"

Nate shrugs. "Yeah, pretty much."

I hit my head back against the headrest.

"Look, I get it," Nate says. "It's awkward talking about . . . feelings. There are tons of things I wish I could say to my brother but can't." He fiddles with the parking break. "It would have been so much easier to talk to him when he was still living across the hall. You and Jenn still live in the same house," Nate says. "At least for now. You might not fix your whole relationship in one night, but if you meet her and talk things out, maybe you can fix what happened between you two today."

"What if she doesn't show up?" I ask. "What if she decides she doesn't want to waste any more time on me?"

He reaches across the center console and gently takes my hand. At first, I don't know what to do, but his fingers are warm against mine, and holding hands feels surprisingly normal.

"April, trust me," he says. "You are worth showing up for."

His words flood me with hope. I look down at our interlaced fingers and breathe out a long, slow breath. "You'll go with me?" I ask. "To meet her?"

"Of course." He sits back and holds out his cell phone. "Here. Find out where she wants to meet."

I take the phone. I expect him to let go of my hand, but he doesn't—he keeps his fingers entwined with mine. First he says he thinks I deserve better than Eric, and now he's holding my hand. Suddenly, it's like I'm sitting next to a complete stranger. A cute, smells-good, actually-returns-my-calls *stranger*.

"I wonder where she would have gone if you didn't call," Nate says absently as I start to dial.

I look up at him. I don't know where she's planning to be at eight. I have absolutely no idea. But as I sit here, phone in hand, it occurs to me that calling to ask her is almost as bad as not showing up. I might as well admit I don't care enough about our relationship to figure out the answer.

I hand the phone back to Nate. "Let's try to figure it out on our own. If it gets too close to eight o'clock and we still haven't figured it out, then we'll call her."

"Works for me."

He starts to let go of my hand so he can shift the car into drive, but I don't let him.

"Hold on," I say. "If I'm gonna do this, I want you to do something too."

"Like what?"

"If I look for Jenn, then you have to promise that tomorrow you'll call Bo."

Nate presses his lips together. "No."

"Come on, you know you miss him. And it'll make your mom feel better too."

Nate stares down at our hands for a long moment, then runs his thumb along mine. It sends a shiver racing up my arm.

"Fine," he says. "But it's almost seven, so we better get started."

His fingers slip away from of mine, and for a moment I'm afraid I've made him angry. But that's not Nate's way. He doesn't pull away or withhold when he doesn't get what he wants.

"Where should we start?" Nate asks as he steers us toward the parking lot exit. "What kind of place would your sister want to go that's important to both of you?"

I run my finger along the dashboard, tracing patterns in the dust. Beside me, Nate waits patiently, the edge of his arm brushing mine as he reaches to turn on the AC. I'm suddenly aware of how close we're sitting, how easy it would be to reach for his hand again—

You're supposed to be thinking about your sister, I scold myself, *not about Nate*. I sit up straight in my seat, close my eyes, and force myself to focus. *Where would she go? What's the one place that has always been meaningful to both of us?* I picture all the things we used to do together before she started high school. All the fun we used to have, especially during those long, hot summer days while Mom and Dad were at work—

"I've got it," I say, and open my eyes. "Turn right."

CHAPTER 26

JENN

I should get up. I've been sitting on the top step, hoping to overhear my parents discussing my fate downstairs in the living room, for the last twenty minutes. But they're not discussing it. They're not discussing *anything*. Instead, they're sitting together watching TV, which might *seem* normal, but is completely bizarre for them because usually they can't agree on what to watch and the whole thing devolves into an argument within a few minutes. But not tonight. Tonight, they're happily watching *Modern Family* reruns. Maybe I should be happy that for once my parents aren't fighting, but it's difficult considering the only reason for the cease-fire is that for once in their lives they're in complete agreement on something—that I am absolutely *not* leaving for Stanford tomorrow morning.

When it all gets to be too much—and my butt begins to hurt from sitting, unmoving, on the hardwood stairs—I slowly make my way down the hall to my room. On the way,

I notice April's door is open and the lights are on. I peek inside to see if she's home, but the room is empty. I'd normally turn off the light and close the door, but instead I step inside.

I've never been in here alone before. I tread carefully as I walk around her room, my fingertips brushing against her paper-strewn desk, her collection of soccer trophies, her unmade bed. I find myself lingering there, next to the nest of sheets and blankets, and before I can change my mind, I kick off my shoes and lie down on her cold sheets. I'm immediately enveloped by the smell of detergent, plus a hint of the apricot antifrizz serum April uses on her curls. The smell is so distinctly my little sister that I'm caught by surprise, and before I even know it's happening, I'm crying.

I don't know what I'm doing—not just here, in April's room, but with my entire life. I'm used to having everything under control. I'm responsible, I have a contingency plan for every scenario, my friends come to *me* with their problems . . . or, they used to, before I started spending all my time with Tom. But now everything is a mess. *I* am a mess.

I hear a noise in the hall and immediately tense. April might not care that I'm in her room, but she's going to be confused when she finds me crying in her bed. But she doesn't come in—no one does. I sit up and wipe my eyes. Where is she, anyway? I figured she'd come back from the store with Mom and Dad, but she's not here. I try to remember if she mentioned doing anything tonight, but the only plan we talked about was my ill-fated dinner.

Except . . . I *do* remember her saying something about meeting at eight o'clock.

Oh, *shit*.

The conversation comes back to me, and I bury my face in a pillow. April's idea is totally ridiculous, and chances are she already forgot all about it. But if she was serious, I'll look like a total asshole if I don't show up.

I get out of bed and head toward my room. The first thing I need to do is find out where she's actually going to be. I grab my cell phone and I'm on the verge of dialing when I realize I have a missed call from Tom. My finger hovers over his name, as if magnetized. I want to call him back. I want to do it so badly that it feels like a physical need. But I know Tom, and once his mind is made up, that's it. It's over. So what is there left to say?

I steel myself, then delete the record of his call and dial April instead. I drum my fingers on my desk as I wait for her to answer, but after ringing a few times, the call goes to voicemail. April never listens to them, so I hang up and try her number again. The phone rings and rings. "Pick up," I mutter. "For once in your life, pick up your phone."

The call goes to voicemail again. *Of course.*

The brass alarm clock by my bed reads 6:50, but it's twenty minutes slow, which means I have just under an hour until we're supposed to meet. *If* we're supposed to meet.

I hurry downstairs, not bothering to say goodbye to my parents as I pass by the living room on my way out the front door. I'm fiddling with my keys, looking for the one to my bike so I can go pick up the car, when I come to an abrupt halt.

Shruthi and Katie are sitting on my driveway in the dark, the only light coming from the streetlight half a block away and their cell phones.

"What are you guys doing here?" I ask. "Shruthi, I thought you were going home."

"I did," she says, "but when I told Katie about the conversation you were having with your parents, she thought we'd better come over in case you needed us."

I grip my keys. I know I told Shruthi about lying to my parents, but I wasn't prepared for her to tell anyone else. And even though it's just Katie, it still feels weird talking about this stuff with anyone but Tom. "That was really nice of you," I say. "Thank you."

"Of course," Shruthi says as she gets to her feet.

Katie gestures at my house. "So, how did it go?" she asks. "Did you tell them?"

"Yeah," I say, even though technically it was *April* who broke the news, not me. "They don't want me to go, and they won't help me pay for all the expenses financial aid doesn't cover."

"That sucks, dude," Katie says.

"Maybe you can transfer to UCLA next semester?" Shruthi asks.

"Maybe," I say, looking back at the house. The idea of living here for another six months makes me feel sick to my stomach, especially after the fights I had today with my parents *and* with April. "I don't want to think about it right now," I say, turning back to my friends. "It's been kind of a long day."

"So what *do* you want to do?" Katie asks.

"This is going to sound weird," I say, gesturing for them to follow me to the car, "but I made this deal with my sister . . ."

CHAPTER 27

APRIL

"It smells like feet," Nate says the moment we walk into the Marina del Rey Ice Rink. "Why would Jenn come *here*?"

"Because we loved it as kids." I spin across the floor, narrowly missing a woman and her husband as they step off the ice. "We did kiddie skating when I was in first grade and she was in third, and we spent almost every day here the summer before she started high school. We couldn't always pay for skates, so we'd just hang out in the stands and people-watch."

I lean over the edge of the rink. Kids of all ages zoom by, while the adults wobble around the rink slowly, clutching each other's hands as they move in fits and starts. I'm underdressed for this freezing skating rink, but I don't care. All I want to do is get out on the ice.

Nate stands next to me, but instead of watching the skaters, he's looking at me. "Why'd you stop coming?"

"Jenn stopped wanting to, then the school year began

and she met Thomas. Once they started dating, it was pretty much the end of us hanging out."

A girl our age skates past, her hands tucked into the pockets in her dress like she's simply strolling down the street. As I watch, she turns and begins to skate backward, a small smile on her face as she navigates the rink. They look nothing alike, but there's something about the way she's smiling, perfectly happy to be here on her own, that would have once reminded me of my sister. But now that I know what it's like for Jenn, working at the store all the time while our parents bring down the house with their arguing, I wonder if she actually *likes* doing stuff on her own after all . . . or if she does it because she thinks she has to.

"Bo and I used to hang out a lot more when we were younger," Nate says. "He was seven years older than me, so of course I thought he was *super* cool."

I turn way from the ice, glad for the distraction. "What did you guys do together?"

"All kinds of stuff. He taught me how to play basketball and video games, and he always defended me when Dad threatened to send me to a Korean after-school program if I didn't stop goofing off in class."

"*You*, goofing off in class?" I say, clutching my chest. "I cannot imagine that."

Nate smiles. "He got busy when he started high school and started caring about different stuff. Like his grades and his friends. And, to my horror, *girls*." He laughs. "He still made time for me, though."

"And now?"

He looks down at his feet. "I don't really know him."

"Yeah," I say. "I know what you mean. I barely know Jenn at all. I mean, I *thought* I did, but after today . . ."

"You do know her, though. You know the stuff that counts."

"I missed a lot, Nate. Like, a *lot*."

"Maybe," he says. "But you also notice a lot too. You thought something was wrong when you saw her in the kitchen yesterday, and you were right." He gestures at the rink. "And you knew she'd come here too."

"No, I *think* she'll come here." The things she said to me in the car, about how I only care about myself, come back to me, and my confidence disappears. "I'm probably wrong."

"Well," Nate says, checking the clock on the wall, "we won't know for forty-five more minutes. What should we do while we wait?"

Another little girl in a pink skating outfit passes by and waves at me. I wave back at her. "We should skate."

I pull Nate toward the rental booth. We pay, then lace up our skates on a narrow bench a few feet away.

"I don't remember how to do this," Nate says when his skates are securely on his feet. He wobbles a few steps and grabs my shoulder to steady himself. "Actually, I don't think I ever knew how to do this."

I stand slowly, careful not to push him off balance. "You know how to Rollerblade, right? It's just like that."

We make our way to the ice, but Nate hesitates at the entrance. "I might fall."

"Come on, you're not going to fall. And even if you do, it won't be that bad."

"Maybe." A smile breaks through the solemn expression on his face. "But I think you should hold my hand. You know, just in case."

"Oh!" I say. "Um, sure. If you want to?"

"I do." He holds out his hand, and for the second time tonight, his warm fingers close over mine.

"Now I'm ready," he says. "Let's go."

We step onto the ice. I'm a little unsteady at first, but then my legs remember how to glide around the rink. Nate takes to it immediately, and soon we're flying past the other skaters, hand in hand. It's exhilarating, and for a few minutes I'm able to forget about everything—about Jenn leaving, our parents fighting, even Eric. All that matters is Nate's hand in mine and the wind in my hair as we whip around the rink, laughing as we dodge and weave our way around the other skaters.

By the time we've gone around the rink three times, my face is sore from smiling. I keep expecting Nate to let go of my hand, especially when we come upon a group of kids skating slowly in the middle of the ice. But instead he speeds up, then turns and skates backward so we're facing each other. Suddenly, our hands aren't the only thing linking us—we're also staring into each other's eyes.

"I'm really sorry about what happened earlier with Eric," he says. "That really sucked."

I nod, but with Nate looking at me the way he is, Eric is

the last thing on my mind. "It's okay. I'd rather be with you anyway."

He looks surprised, and I realize my mistake. "Oh my gosh, that's not what I meant. What I was trying to say is, I'd rather be *here*. Not with you."

"So you *don't* want to be with me?" he asks.

"No, I *do*, it's just . . . I didn't . . ." I search for the right thing to say, but the words don't come. Because it turns out, I meant exactly what I said.

I only want to be with Nate.

"April?" he asks, his voice low and soft despite the noise around us.

I swallow and lift my chin. If I'm going to embarrass myself, I might as well get it over with. "I want to be here," I say. "With you. No one else."

Nate slows down so we're only a few inches apart. We're still skating, but so slowly that it's more like dancing. "You don't want to be with Eric?"

I shake my head. "Not anymore. And not just because he's seeing other people."

"Then why?" Nate asks.

We continue to skate, hand in hand, as I think through what I'm trying to say. "When we first started hanging out, it made me feel special that someone as popular as Eric was into me. But I felt nervous around him too." I remember the ride he gave me and Jenn earlier today, how abruptly his mood changed the moment I took Jenn's side. "It sometimes felt like he might stop liking me if I said the wrong thing. I didn't realize it until today, but I've spent a lot of time trying to please him because I was worried that if I didn't, he might lose interest."

"That's not right," Nate says. "You should never have to worry about that."

"I know," I say. "And when I'm with you, I don't have to worry about anything, because I know you'll like me no matter what."

"I will," Nate says, pulling me close. "I always have."

I stare up into his face, the whole world shrinking down to the space between us. "So what does that mean?" I ask.

"It means I want to be with you too, April."

My heart races in my chest, faster than it ever has before. What if things don't work out between us? If it gets complicated, I could lose his friendship forever. Is being with Nate worth the risk?

He smiles, and the dimple in his left cheek appears. I've seen it a million and one times, but standing here, in his arms, it feels like the first.

Yes, Nate's worth it. He absolutely is.

I pull him into the middle of the rink, where people aren't skating so much as standing, and I put my arms around his neck. Strangers continue to circle around us, but as I look into Nate's dark brown eyes, everything else disappears. "Say it again."

"I want to be with you," he says.

My breath catches in my chest. "Again, please."

He laughs. "April, I want to be with you. I want to be with—"

I push forward onto the front tips of my skates and press my lips to his. He freezes for a second, as surprised as I am by what I just did. Then his lips part and he pulls me closer. The kiss deepens as his hands start to creep down my back, and my heart races all over again.

"Not the place for that," a man says as he skates past us.

I pull away, and Nate immediately starts laughing. "Sorry, sir!" he calls to the man's back as he skates away. But as soon as he's gone, Nate pulls me toward him again and leans his forehead against mine. "I don't want to rush this," he says. "I know you and Eric—"

"Forget Eric," I say. "Kiss me again."

He cups my face and leans down, but before he has a chance to do anything more, the overhead lights flash and a voice comes on over the loudspeaker.

"Attention, skaters! The rink is closing for a private party. Please exit the ice, and have a great evening!"

"No!" I exclaim, pulling away. "We haven't found Jenn yet!"

I skate to the edge of the rink and hop onto the side so I can search the exiting crowd for my sister.

"I don't see her, do you?" I ask Nate when he joins me.

"Not yet," he says, just as a group of ten-year-olds explodes onto the ice. One of them careens toward us, just narrowly missing Nate. "But I think we better get out of the way."

I follow him off the ice. Once we're clear, Nate checks his watch. "It's only seven forty-five. She might not be here yet."

He's right—she could still be on her way. But she could

also be somewhere else entirely. *Why the hell did I suggest this stupid idea?*

"Do you want to wait outside for her?" Nate asks as we head toward the benches to take off our skates. "Or maybe you should just call her?"

I slump onto the bench. "Yeah, I guess. Can I use your phone?"

Nate hands me his cell. "Go for it."

I tap the screen, but it doesn't light up. I try turning it on, but still nothing happens. "I cannot believe this."

"What?"

"It's dead."

"Seriously?" Nate takes his phone back, fiddles with it for a second, then groans. "I must have forgotten to charge it last night."

"Great," I say as I yank off my right skate and drop it on the floor. "That's just *great*."

"Don't get upset," he says. "We can still fix this."

"There is no 'we,'" I snap. "If I don't find Jenn, she's going to be mad at *me*, not you."

Nate jerks back like I've slapped him. "I'm just trying to help."

"I know," I say. "I'm sorry. I'm just so frustrated. This whole day has been one mess after another, and even though this meet-at-eight-o'clock thing is stupid, it feels like the only way to make things right with her." I yank off my second skate and slide my feet back into my shoes. "She's probably not going to even bother showing up. If I were her, I probably wouldn't."

The door to the skate rental booth swings open, and a tall man in khaki shorts appears, his long, hairy legs unfolding like an erector set as he steps through the door. He looks down his nose at the swarms of people taking off skates and finishing snacks, then cups his hands around his mouth. "The rink is *closed*," he barks, his voice so loud the little girl on the bench next to me jumps. "Grab your stuff and *get out*."

"Oh my god," I say. "It's Big Pete."

"Big *who*?" Nate asks.

"Big Pete. He's been the manager here for years. I totally forgot about him." I duck down, then peer at Big Pete over Nate's shoulder. "Now I remember—*he's* the reason Jenn and I stopped coming here. He noticed we were hanging around every day and not spending any money, and he banned us from the rink!"

"Sounds like a jerk," Nate says.

"Totally. After he banned us, Jenn said that was fine because we were never coming back anyway—" I freeze. "Oh my god."

"What?"

"Jenn said we were never coming back!"

Nate's eyes go wide. "So that means—"

"This isn't the right place!" I look down at Nate's feet. He's still got one skate on. "Come on, take that off. We've got to hurry."

"Do you know where we should go next?"

"I'm not sure," I say as he pulls on his shoes. We both stand and head for the exit. "But we only have fifteen minutes—"

"Hey!" Big Pete calls to us. "You two better pick those skates up and return them or you won't be welcome back here."

I go back to the bench, grab the skates, and plop them onto the rental counter just as Big Pete steps back inside the booth. "I'm already not welcome back," I say, pointing to a photo of my sister and me pinned to the corkboard behind him. "See?"

Big Pete pulls the photo off the board and squints at it. "That's you?" he asks.

I reach across the counter and snatch the photo out of his hands. My sister and I are standing in front of the same booth I'm currently leaning against, our arms crossed. Jenn's scowling at the camera, and I'm sticking my tongue out. At the top of the photo, in permanent marker, Big Pete has scrawled BANNED.

"We got Boba after this," I say, smiling. "It was Jenn's first time having it, and she almost choked on a tapioca ball. We laughed so hard."

"Isn't that nice," Big Pete sneers.

"Yeah," I say, smiling down at the photo. "It was."

I turn to Nate. "We used to come here because it was too hot to hang outside, but the reason we were outside in the first place was because we had to get away from my parents." I look down at the photo again, and grin. "This wasn't the only place we used to go to get away, though. It wasn't even our first choice."

"Sounds like you figured out where we're going next."

"Damn right."

We start to walk away, but Big Pete calls after us.

"Wait a minute," he says. "You have to give that picture back! Banned once means—"

"Banned for life!" I say, wagging the photo in the air. "I remember."

"Bye, Big Pete!" Nate calls as he waves. "Have a good night!"

Big Pete splutters something, but we don't hear it. We're too busy pushing through the exit doors and hurrying out into the night.

CHAPTER 28

JENN

This is the place," I say. "I can feel it."

We're parked next to Culver City High School, staring at the empty soccer field. I haven't been here since graduation a few months ago, and already the place feels small and far away, like I'm peering at it from years in the future instead of through an old chain-link fence.

"I'm telling you, it doesn't feel right," Shruthi says. "I know April likes soccer, but you said this was supposed to be a place that's important to *both* of you."

"It is, but . . ." I hesitate, searching for the right words. I don't want to sound like I'm throwing April under the bus, but Shruthi and Katie don't know her like I do. "Let's just say, she doesn't always see other people quite as clearly as she thinks she does."

Katie snorts in the back seat.

"What?" I ask, looking at her in the rearview mirror.

She looks out the window. "Nothing."

"If you have something to say, say it."

Shruthi rubs her temples. "Quit it, both of you."

"She started it," Katie grumbles.

I spin in my seat to face her. "I did *not*."

Shruthi unbuckles her seat belt and throws open her door. "You two can keep fighting if you want to, but I'm going to check the field."

I kill the engine and we all get out. The field is flooded with light even though it's a Saturday night in August. I don't even want to think about how much money they're wasting on electricity.

"She's not here," Katie says when we reach the field.

"Not *yet*," I snap.

Shruthi sits cross-legged on the grass. "Tell me again why you think this is where she'll be."

I pat the grass to make sure it's dry, then sit next to her. "She's really into soccer. She even brought me to Venice Beach today because it's where we went to celebrate her getting onto the JV team."

Katie sits beside me. "Why didn't she bring you here earlier today, then? To the field where she actually made the team?"

"I'm not sure," I admit. "Maybe because this isn't as fun as the boardwalk?"

"Or maybe," Shruthi says, "it's because soccer wasn't the point. Celebrating with *you* was."

I squeeze my knees to my chest. If Shruthi's right, then that explains why April looked so bummed today when I couldn't remember why Muscle Beach mattered to her. But how was I supposed to remember something that happened so long ago? She can't expect me to keep every single little detail of our lives recorded in my memory.

Except . . . that's exactly what I expected *her* to do. It's why I was so pissed today—first at the Ferris wheel, and later at lunch.

Apparently, April's not the only one who can be unreasonable.

I look around the empty soccer field and sigh. "You're right, Shruthi. This isn't the right place. Let's go."

We head back to the car and climb inside. "We only have twenty minutes left," I say as I start the engine. "There's no way we're going to figure this out."

"I still think we should have stayed longer at Van Leeuwen," Katie mutters in the back seat. "At least long enough to get a sundae."

Shruthi pulls a small spiral notebook and a mechanical pencil from her purse and crosses off *soccer field* from the short list we made before we left my house. *Van Leeuwen* and *Westfield mall* have already suffered the same fate.

"Is there anything left?" I ask Shruthi.

"Just Lindberg Park."

"She won't be there," I say. "Trust me."

Shruthi tips her head to the side. "But you said that's where you made the pact when you were kids. How can she *not* remember that, when she's the one who remembered the pact in the first place?"

I start the car in lieu of an answer. I may have been wrong to expect April to perfectly remember every little detail of our lives, but I'm not wrong about this.

"Let's go to the park anyway," Shruthi says. She double-taps the pad with the eraser end of her mechanical pencil. "It's five minutes from here, so if it doesn't feel right, we can leave."

"Fine," I say. "But it's a waste of five minutes."

I pull away from the curb, and we ride to the park in silence. I try not to, but I find myself glancing at Katie in the rearview mirror every few seconds. She's clearly angry about something. I look at Shruthi, hoping for a clue as to what's wrong with Katie, or at least a sympathetic eye roll, but she's staring straight ahead, her arms tightly crossed and her lips pursed. It's the same face she was making earlier tonight at her house.

Are they both mad at me?

"It looks pretty empty," Shruthi says when I pull up to the park.

"I told you," I mutter.

"But," she says, opening the door, "we might as well get out and look around."

We climb out of the car and cross the parking lot toward the playground. The park is deserted, the only noise coming from our feet crunching across the sand as we step into the play area. I circle the jungle gym and head for the swings.

"This feels right," Shruthi says as she leans against the bright blue slide sticking out of a piece of playground equipment. "I think she'll come. Don't you?"

A few minutes ago, I was sure she wouldn't. But sitting here now, I'm suddenly not as confident. April and I did indeed come here on the day of the pact—in fact, we spent most of the day hanging out under the blue slide Shruthi is leaning against at this very minute, eating ice cream. But even though there would be a certain amount of poetry to April choosing to meet me here, a part of me hopes she doesn't, since it would pretty much ruin the whole let's-meet-somewhere-that-has-a-positive-memory-attached-to-it-for-*both*-of-us thing.

"If we're staying," Katie says, "we might as well get comfortable."

She climbs onto a piece of castle-shaped play equipment and sits. Below her, Shruthi leans against the slide.

We sit in silence, waiting. I keep checking my phone, but I have no calls from April, and Nate hasn't returned the call I made from the mall parking lot. Either they're not together, or she's not coming.

I look over at my friends just as Shruthi says something softly to Katie, who shakes her head in response. Shruthi says something again, and they both smile. I wrap my hands around the metal rings of the swing and try to pretend not to care that they're whispering to each other *again*. But when Shruthi giggles, then quickly covers her mouth, I lose my cool. "Do you guys need some privacy?" I ask. "'Cause I can go."

Shruthi immediately looks apologetic, but Katie crosses her arms. "I know you're stressed right now, but don't take it out on us."

"I'm not," I say. "I'm just tired of you guys whispering like I'm not even here. It's rude to leave someone out like that."

Katie mutters, "Hypocrite."

"How am I a hypocrite?" I demand. "Is this about Stanford? Because it's really none of your business that I didn't tell my parents."

"It's not that," Katie says. "You've been distant for months, and then today at lunch . . ." She shakes her head, but doesn't continue.

Shruthi sighs and joins me on the swings. "You know we care about you and want you to be happy," Shruthi says. "Right?"

I wrap my arms around myself. "Right."

"Good. Then you know what I'm about to say is coming from a place of love." She takes a deep breath and folds her hands in her lap. "Today at lunch, you were a total jackass."

I suck in a sharp breath. Beside me, Katie laughs. "Dude," she says. "I don't think I've ever heard you curse."

"That's because you don't speak Hindi," Shruthi says, waving her off. "But, Jenn, I'm serious. You were really unfair to us."

"I already apologized to you about lunch," I say as Katie comes down the slide to stand next to Shruthi.

"You didn't apologize to *me*," Katie says. "And you basically called us bad friends, just because we're living together. What's so horrible about that?"

"It wasn't just that," I say. "You guys are leaving me behind."

"We're not leaving you behind," Shruthi says. "We're going to college. If anyone is doing the leaving, it's you." She and Katie exchange another look. "I know this is a bad time to bring this up because you and Tom just broke up, but you guys have been a closed circuit this year. We only saw you in class, never on the weekends. And like Katie said at lunch, every time we've tried to talk to you about the future, you've gotten quiet and refused to discuss it."

I twist my hands in my lap. "Yeah," I say. "I know."

"Tell her what you told me," Shruthi says to Katie. "After lunch."

Katie grimaces. "You didn't hug us. You just said goodbye, and went out to the car with April, like it was any other day. I thought you were pissed about our argument at lunch, but Shruthi insisted you were just distracted, since you probably still had a lot of stuff to do before moving. So we waved at you from across the parking lot. But instead of waving back . . . you pretended not to notice."

I want to jump out of my swing and wrap my arms around them both—it's the only way I know how to apologize for being so stupid and thoughtless. But before I can get up the courage, Katie says, "There's more." Her gaze drops to the sand at her feet. "On the way home, I just kept thinking, *Maybe this is it. Maybe she's not just mad, or busy, or distracted. Maybe she doesn't want to be friends with us anymore.*"

I grip the chain of the swing. "Oh my gosh, *never*," I say. "I just got so caught up in the secret I was keeping that I stopped paying attention to anything else."

As the words leave my mouth, a horrible thought occurs to me: Is this what Tom was talking about?

"What's wrong?" Shruthi asks. "You look upset."

"It's nothing," I say immediately.

"Don't do that," Katie says. "Please, Jenn. You've been shutting us out for months. Please don't do it now."

I drag my flat through the sand beneath the swing, not meeting Katie's eye. "Do you guys think I'm self-centered?"

"Why in the world would you ask that?" Shruthi asks.

"It's something Tom said when he was breaking up with me. He said I don't listen to other people. All I care about is what's going on with me." I feel tears coming, but I press on. "And now you guys are saying I've been ignoring you, and then there's the whole thing with not telling my parents the truth, and how I treated April today and . . . what if he's right? What if *I'm* the selfish one?" The first tear rolls down my cheek, followed quickly by another.

"You absolutely are *not*," Katie says fiercely. "You give more of yourself than anyone I've ever met. Sometimes *too* much."

"But you just said I haven't been around for you guys lately—"

"Yeah, and that sucked," Katie says. "But it doesn't mean you're a selfish person. It just means you made a mistake."

"And as for your parents," Shruthi says, "you've been putting your needs second for *years*. Just because you're tired of doing that doesn't mean you're some kind of monster." She shakes her head. "That reasoning is simplistic at best. It's also extremely ironic." I must look as confused as I feel, because she continues. "Tom's accusing you of not listening, and of not talking to your parents because you're selfish. Right?"

"Right . . ."

"Then what does it say about *him* that he gave you absolutely no warning whatsoever that he was unhappy, and then ended things without giving you a chance to defend yourself, or, I don't know, fix things between the two of you?"

Katie takes a seat on the swing to my left. "She's got a point."

"Maybe," I say.

"No, *definitely*," Katie says. "You can't just expect people to read your mind. You have to *talk* to them. You also have to give them a chance to be there for you."

She takes my hand, making it clear that even though she's talking about Tom, she's talking a little bit about her and Shruthi, too. But as we sit there, holding hands, I realize the person this applies to more than anyone isn't the three of them, or even my parents. It's April.

I've been so focused on everything else that's going on that I've missed something truly obvious: This entire day was about my sister trying to be here for me. She even stuck it out after I admitted I'd lied to her. But instead of appreciating everything she's done, I've been awful to her. When she didn't get every little thing right, I held it against her. It never even occurred to me that it might be forgivable that she had forgotten a few things over the years, or that maybe she had been too young to realize them in the first place. I never gave her the benefit of the doubt. I assumed the worst.

Just like I'm doing now.

"You guys," I say. "The park . . . it's not the right place."

"Are you sure?" Shruthi asks.

"I think so. I figured she had forgotten everything about the day we made the pact except the good stuff, so it would have made sense that she'd come here. But I was underestimating her."

I get off the swing and start to pace back and forth through the sand. "All day she's been picking stuff that I thought was all about her, but I've been missing the point. She hasn't been choosing places just because they're fun. She's been picking places where we've actually, you know . . . talked. Connected."

"I still don't understand why it can't be here," Shruthi says, gesturing to the park around us. "It seems like this should be the perfect place."

I come to an abrupt stop. "We spent the day here, but then we went home—to the one place we always spent time together when we wanted to get away. That's where we made the pact. Not here."

Katie grins. "Did you just figure out where she is?"

I smile back. "I think so."

"Then let's go!" Shruthi says. "I'll get the car."

I check my phone. It's already 7:55.

"No time—there's still too much traffic. I'm just going

to run." I turn to leave, then face my friends again. "Thank you guys so much for helping me. I know I need to be better about—"

"Tell us later!" Katie exclaims. "Go!"

I hug them both, my arms flung wide around them, then take off running.

CHAPTER 29

APRIL

ove!" I yell out the window. "It's Saturday night! All you people should be home or at a club or something. Not in your stupid cars!"

"We're less than ten minutes away," Nate says as we inch forward in traffic even though the light ahead is green. "You're going to be on time." The light turns yellow, then red, and we come to a stop. "*Maybe* a minute or two late," Nate amends. "Max."

"Jenn is never late. Ever." I cross my arms, then uncross them. The clock on the dashboard clicks forward another minute. 7:52.

"What if I'm wrong?" I ask. "What if she's somewhere else?"

"I don't think she will be, but even if she is, it'll be okay."

"No, it won't. If I'm wrong and she's somewhere else, I might as well bake her a big cake that says, SORRY I DON'T CARE ABOUT YOU ENOUGH TO FIGURE THIS OUT."

The light turns green. Nate changes lanes, and we speed forward. "You can't think that way," he says. "I'm sure Jenn isn't."

"Trust me, that's *exactly* how she's thinking." I cross my arms again. "I screwed up so many times today. I don't want to do it again."

Nate comes to a stop at yet another red light and turns to me. "Even if this *is* the wrong place, and even if Jenn *does* give you a hard time about it, that doesn't mean you're a screwup, or a bad person, or any of the other terrible things you're always saying about yourself. You need to believe that."

I take his hand and give it a squeeze, but I don't say anything. Because even though my head tells me he's probably right, my heart isn't quite so sure.

I check the dash again. 7:54.

"We're not going to make it," I say.

Nate tightens his grip on the steering wheel. "Yes, we are."

The light turns green, and Nate punches the gas. We surge into the intersection, and Nate cuts in front of oncoming traffic to turn left. A few cars honk, including a police cruiser, but we're already flying down a side street. I turn around in my seat, but the police car is miraculously not real—it's just somebody driving a repurposed black-and-white Chevy.

We turn left onto our street, and Nate speeds down the block. We're almost there—I can see my house—when Mrs.

Iniguez steps into the crosswalk up ahead with her new puppy. Nate slams on the brakes. "Shit."

Mrs. Iniguez wags a finger at us and continues to cross *slowly*.

"Hurry up," I mutter under my breath. "For the love of dogs, *please* hurry up."

She continues to walk at a snail's pace. "I think she's doing this on purpose," Nate says through gritted teeth. "I saw her jogging less than a week ago."

7:57.

Mrs. Iniguez finally clears the crosswalk, and Nate punches the gas. Two seconds later, we park in front of my house and jump out of the car.

"Go, go, go!" Nate cries. "I'm right behind you!"

I sprint up the driveway, praying that the door is unlocked so I don't have to fumble for my keys. But I don't have to worry—my dad opens it before I get there.

"There you are," he says, and holds up my cell phone. "You left this at the store—"

"Thanks!" I say, snatching the phone out of his hand.

"Hey!" he says as I continue into the house, Nate right on my heels. "Where are you guys going?"

"No time!" I call over my shoulder as we race up the stairs and into the bathroom. "Help me with this window," I say to Nate. "It sticks."

Together, we push it open, and I throw my leg over the windowsill. Then I step out.

The roof is just as I remember it. Dusty stucco stretches

thirty feet in front of me, studded by an old TV antenna, a half-deflated soccer ball, a Frisbee, and two folding chairs. The only thing *not* up here is Jenn.

"She's not here," I say as Nate steps onto the roof.

"She's not here *yet*."

We walk over to the pair of grubby folding chairs Jenn and I dragged up here years ago and sit. Los Angeles stretches out before us, a carpet of lights extending all the way to the mountains to the east and the ocean to the west. Jenn's right. This is almost exactly the same view as from the stairs.

I check my dad's phone. 7:59. One minute to go.

"What if she's not coming?" I ask. "What if this is the wrong place?"

Nate takes the phone from me and puts it aside. "She'll be here. Have a little faith in her."

I take a deep breath and turn back to the view below us. I've been all over the city today, first trying to cheer up my sister, and then trying to convince her to stay. But again and again I've gotten it wrong. That's what Nate doesn't understand—it's not that I don't have faith in Jenn. It's that I don't have faith in *me*.

"Please, Jenn," I whisper. "Please."

CHAPTER 30

APRIL

It's 8:05.

"She's not coming."

I close my eyes, shutting out the city lights. I'm suddenly exhausted, so I lean sideways and put my head on Nate's shoulder.

"I'm sorry," he says quietly. "I really thought she'd be here."

He waits for me to reply, but there's nothing to say. I hug my knees to my chest.

"Can I get you anything?" he asks. "Are you hungry?"

I cringe at the pity in his voice—it just makes me feel worse. "Can I have some tea?" I ask, just to give him something to do. "Please?"

"Sure." He kisses the top of my head. "Be right back."

He stands and walks toward the window. I watch him step through, then I turn back around. I've only been on the roof for a few minutes, but it feels like I've been sitting here all day, waiting for my sister. I thought today was about trying to convince her to cheer up, and later, to stay. But as I sit here, staring out at the city with my chest aching, I realize what I've really wanted was for her to *want* to be here. Not because of Los Angeles. Not because of the store. Not even because of our parents. I wanted her to stay because I needed her, and I wanted that to matter. I wanted to be reason enough.

CHAPTER 31

JENN

My lungs are going to explode.

When this is over, I'll start doing cardio. I'll go to the gym three times a week. Hell, I'll *live* at the gym if the universe gives me the strength to keep running just a little farther.

I round the corner, and our house comes into view up ahead. Ignoring the ache in my side, I put on a burst of speed. April is there, I know it. And if I can just keep running a little longer, I'll make it on time. For the first time today, I'll be there for *her* instead of the other way around.

I reach the house and fly up the driveway and through the front door.

. . . and nearly collide with my dad.

"Whoa there," he says. "Where's the fire?"

"Can't talk," I gasp, clutching the banister. "Have to find April."

Nate is at the top of the stairs, disappointment written across his face. "You're late."

"I can't be," I say as I continue up the stairs. "It's only—"

"It's 8:07," he says, glancing at the grandfather clock outside April's bedroom. "You were supposed to meet at eight."

My stomach sinks, taking every ounce of energy I have left with it. "Is she out there?" I ask.

He steps to the side in answer, and I continue climbing, taking the remaining stairs two at a time like April always does, before hurrying down the hall and into the bathroom. Luckily, the window is still open, so I don't have to ask Nate for help. I simply step through and find myself in the one place I should have known to come from the start.

April is seated on the other side of the roof in one of our old folding chairs, facing the city. But instead of looking out, she's hunched over, her face in her hands. The sight of her there sends a fresh wave of guilt through me.

"April?" I say quietly, so as not to startle her. "Are you okay?"

She spins around in her chair, her face lit up with surprise. "You came!"

"Of course," I say as I cross the roof. "I'm sorry I'm late, though. To be honest, I had a little bit of trouble figuring out where you were going to be."

Her expression turns stony. "Harder to come up with something *meaningful* than you thought, huh?"

I stop short. "Yes," I say. "It was."

She nods, apparently satisfied, and turns back to the city.

I hesitate, one hand on the back of the second folding chair, unsure how to proceed. Should I apologize again? Should I explain what happened? Or should I just leave her alone until she's ready to talk?

"I thought you weren't coming," she says. "I thought you were still angry at me for manipulating you, so you decided to teach me a lesson or something."

"I'd never do that," I say, but even as the words come out of my mouth I know they aren't true. That sounds *exactly* like something I'd do.

April glances at me. "Where did you look?"

I'm tempted to pretend I checked out a bunch of places that were totally special and just happened to be wrong. But April will be able to tell I'm lying, and that'll make everything worse. So instead, I tell her the truth. "I went to the soccer field because you like soccer, and to Van Leeuwen because you like ice cream, and to the mall because you like . . . actually, I don't know why I went there. Because you like shopping, I guess."

April shakes her head. "Tonight wasn't supposed to be about what *I* like. It was supposed to be about *us*."

"I know," I say. "I'm sorry. I really am."

"It's fine," she says. "I probably don't have a right to complain after all the shitty stuff I did to you today anyway. I was a total bitch."

I turn the second folding chair so it's facing her and sit down. "April, listen to me. Forgetting that you puked at six years old or that nobody came to my seventh-grade birthday party doesn't make you a bitch, nor does trying to get me to climb some stairs. And as for what you said about my friends . . ." I take a deep breath and let it out slowly. "It really hurt me, but I understand why you said it."

I know she's waiting for me to continue, but suddenly I'm nervous. Despite everything that's gone wrong today, April and I have both ended up on this roof together. We could call a truce and let it go at that. But sitting up here with her, where we've spent so much time together, I'm realizing I don't want a truce. I want us to be close again, like we used to be.

"I have been so angry," I say at last, the words escaping like air from a balloon. "For the last three years I've worked at the store almost every single day, and Mom and Dad are barely ever there even though it's *their* store. And then when they *do* come in, they spend the entire time arguing, which is even worse because it means I have to run the business *and* make sure they don't kill each other. It's like all I am to them is an employee and a therapist. There's no room for *me*."

"That's awful," April says.

"It is," I agree. "But no matter how badly I wanted to get out of here, I should have thought about the effect my leaving would have on you, and how much worse I was making it by lying. I'm really, really sorry I didn't tell you sooner."

"It's okay," she says. "I'm sorry I didn't realize how much pressure you've been under. I mean, I knew they fought a lot, but I had no idea things were *this* bad."

"But how could you not know?" I ask as gently as I can.

"You see them fight at home. You must have realized it would be the same at the store."

April looks down at her hands. "Maybe I didn't *want* to know. It's not like I could do anything about it."

"You could have helped me talk to them—"

"I did! Back when you and Tom first started dating, I was the one who had to deal with them because you were never home."

I try to think back, to visualize all the times I helped Mom and Dad at the store, or stepped in when they were fighting. But all I remember is how it felt to be falling for Tom.

"At first I thought maybe I was just talking to them the wrong way," April continues, "like maybe I needed to try a different approach or something. But I think the real problem was—*is*—they don't care what I think."

I want to tell her that's not true . . . but I don't. I'm done assuming I know what April's gone through. If today has taught me anything, it's that neither of us knows each other as well as we thought we did.

"So I stopped trying," April says. "The honeymoon phase wore off between you and Tom, so you were around more. Plus, you were better at it anyway." She scowls. "You're better at *everything*. You're basically perfect."

"I'm not," I say. "Just look at how badly I've screwed everything up this time! I lied, not just about Stanford, but about why I wanted to get the hell out of here in the first place. What you said in the car was exactly right—I should have just talked to them. Who knows, if I had been honest with them from the beginning, maybe this whole situation would be different." I shake my head. "If I had even *once* told them the truth about all the fighting, maybe their marriage wouldn't be such a mess."

"Don't put that on yourself," April says, leaning forward in her chair. "You did the best you could to help them. They're adults, and you shouldn't have to take care of them. It should be the other way around."

There's a noise from inside the house, and we both turn to look. Nate is halfway through the window. "Sorry," he says, standing up. "I didn't mean to interrupt. But I brought you both some red wine I stole from my house. I know you asked for tea, April, but I thought wine might be, uh, more helpful given the circumstances."

He reaches back inside for three mugs, then carries them across the roof to where we're sitting. "I figured it'd be easier to sneak it past your dad if it looked like hot chocolate or something," he says.

"Smooth," I say, accepting a mug. I turn back to April and realize she's grinning at him, so bright and huge that it's like a light has been turned on. I look back to Nate, and he's looking at her the same way.

"What's going on?" I ask.

April puts her mug down on the ground. "You know how you said Eric likes to go out with a lot of people at once?"

"Yeah . . ."

"Well, you were right," she says. "Nate and I went for ice cream at Van Leeuwen—you weren't *totally* wrong about where to look for me, by the way—and we saw him there with another girl."

"Oh, April," I say. "I'm so sorry."

"Thanks," April says. "But it's okay, because it turns out he's not the person I want to be with anyway."

She looks to Nate, who holds up his mug. "Surprise?"

"No way!" I say, looking back and forth between them. "Oh my gosh, that's amazing! You guys are adorable together."

"Thanks," April says, flushing. "It's not official or anything, though—"

"Wait, it's not?" Nate asks.

April goes still. "I mean . . . it can be? If you want?"

"I totally want," Nate says. "For sure."

April grins again, and I shake my head. "You guys are such nerds."

"Speaking of nerds," April says, picking up her wine again, "where's Thomas?"

The sound of his name hits me like a punch, but I breathe through it. I'm going to have to get used to this, so I might as well start now. "We broke up."

April's face falls. "No way! Are you okay?"

"I don't know, to be honest. It's still really new. I need to sit with it for a while."

April nods but doesn't push further. Instead, Nate grabs a bucket to sit on, and the three of us stare out at the city, drinking wine and breathing in the night air. I feel a rush of relief, as if I've been walking around with a broken bone that's finally been reset. But even though I'm happy to have been honest with April, clearing the air has left room for me to worry about the *other* thing that's been in the back of my mind ever since I left the house a few hours ago—college.

"I told them about Stanford," I say. "And about how I needed them to help me pay for housing and other stuff."

April looks at me sharply. "And?"

"They said no."

"That's it? Just 'no'?"

"They told me the same thing as last time: They need me to be here to help with the store."

"But you hate it!" April protests. "You hate working there, and you hate working for *them*. Did you tell them that?"

"I can't, April. Can you imagine how it'd make them feel? *Hey, your fighting makes me miserable and the only thing that will help is if I leave Los Angeles entirely.* And besides, they said the only way they can handle the store without me is if you work there every day after school. And I know I was a jerk about it earlier, but I get it now—you can't do it, and you shouldn't have to."

"But that's still not fair."

"No," I agree, "it isn't."

For a moment it seems like that's going to be the end of it, but then April jumps to her feet. "Come on. We're going downstairs."

"Why?" Nate and I both ask.

"Because you're going to tell them the truth," she tells me.

She holds out her hand to help me up, but I don't take it. "There's no point," I argue. "It's not going to change the way they feel. They already made that perfectly clear."

"Maybe not," she says, "but it might change how *you* feel."

I chew on my bottom lip, considering. If I tell them the truth, it's going to hurt their feelings, and it'll probably make living here even worse. But if I don't, there's no chance of anything ever changing. And more than working in the store, more than staying in LA, that's what I'm afraid of—that it's going to be like this forever.

"Okay," I say, taking her hand. "Let's go."

She pulls me to my feet, and we head inside. Together.

CHAPTER 32

JENN

We find our parents in the kitchen, making a late dinner like they always do when April and I aren't home to eat with them. For some reason, cooking is the one thing they can do together without fighting. I think it has to do with all the fire and sharp objects—they must subconsciously realize it's best not to argue near weapons.

"Where have you three been?" Mom asks, noticing us in the doorway.

"We were upstairs," April says. "On the roof."

Dad turns to us. "You know we don't want you going up there," he says. "It's not safe."

"Sorry," I say.

April rolls her eyes, but I notice a smile tugging at the corner of her mouth. *Wuss*, she mouths.

"Nate, are you staying for dinner?" Mom asks. "You're more than welcome. There's going to be plenty."

"Thanks, but I've got to get back home," he says. "Catch you later, April."

They stare at each other for a moment, then she gives him a quick kiss and pushes him out the front door.

"Interesting," Dad observes. Mom just smiles.

I take a seat at the breakfast bar. April joins me, her cheeks flushed, but then she tips her head in Mom and Dad's direction, and I know she's back to thinking about the problem at hand: talking to them about how much I hate working at the store. Part of me wishes she would kick the conversation off, since it was her idea to talk to them, but a bigger part knows I need to do this for myself.

"Mom, Dad," I say, my voice loud enough that they both jump, "I have something to tell you."

Dad puts down the knife he was using. "What's up?"

I take a deep breath to prepare myself. There's a good chance they're going to get defensive, or act like they have no idea what I'm talking about and try to change the subject. They might even give me some kind of lame excuse. But it's like I learned in the debate class Shruthi and I took junior year—it's okay if you're forced to refute a counterargument or dodge a curveball as long as you get back on track as soon as possible.

Except there's also another possibility: They could *listen*. If that happens, then they'll know the truth. They'll be forced to stare it in the face and grapple not only with how they've been making me feel, but how dysfunctional things are between them. I know that's the whole point of telling them—to clear the air so we can fix things. But sitting here, watching them making dinner, I'm not sure I can do it. I've spent so long keeping the peace between them. If I shatter it now and everything falls apart, it'll be my fault.

Everyone is watching me, waiting. I can feel their expectation, especially April's. God, I don't want to let her down. But I can't do this. I can't.

"Jenn?" she says.

"I'm sorry," I whisper. "I can't."

"That's okay," she says. "I can."

Before I fully grasp what she means, April turns in her seat to face Mom and Dad. "It's not fair for you to make Jenn stay here and work at the store. She hates it there, and it's your fault."

Dad jerks back, almost like he was slapped. "Excuse me?"

"She didn't mean that," I say quickly. "She was—"

"I *did* mean that," April says. "You guys are always fighting, and it's not just screwing up the business. It's screwing up Jenn's life."

I drop my head into my hands.

"What is your sister talking about?" Dad asks.

I take a long, steadying breath. *I can do this.* "The thing is," I say slowly, "you guys are almost never in the store. And when you are, you're always fighting. Even in front of customers."

"That's not true," Mom says. "We may *disagree* from time to time, but we never let strangers see us do it."

"Well, *I* don't," Dad says. "But your mother definitely has a habit of raising her voice in public."

Mom slams the tomato she's holding onto the counter with such force I'm surprised it doesn't explode. "Me?" she says. "You're the one who is constantly losing your temper—"

"Stop!" I shout. "This is exactly what I'm talking about. One of you will say something rude, and the other will jump at the chance to respond. Then before I know it, you're screaming at each other. It happened yesterday, when that lady came in for a lamp."

"And today," April adds. "Two guys came in while we were in the office. You were fighting so loudly that they left."

Dad clears his throat. "That's . . . that's good to know. But how your mother and I handle our relationship isn't really your concern—"

"It's *absolutely* our concern," April says. "Who knows, if you two would stop fucking fighting all the time—"

"April!" Dad barks. "Watch your language."

"*Sorry,*" she says. "What I meant is, if you stopped fighting, the business would probably do better. We might even make enough so you could hire extra help. Then Jenn wouldn't have to work at the store."

"It's not that simple," Mom says.

"Maybe not," I interject, "but it's not really the point I'm trying to make either." I take another steadying breath. This is it. There's no more beating around the bush. "I've always wanted to go away to college," I say carefully, "but it's not just because I wanted to live somewhere else. It's because I don't want to live *here*."

"Why not?" Dad says, his voice full of surprise. "You love LA."

"I do," I say. "Especially after today."

Beneath the breakfast bar, April reaches over and gives my hand a squeeze. I squeeze back.

"But I'm constantly caught in the middle of your fighting," I continue, "and I can't do it anymore. I can't take care of you *and* your business."

Mom's face falls, and my confidence falters. I don't want to hurt them. I really, really don't. But I think about what April said on the roof, and I push forward. "It's not my responsibility to take care of you guys."

The kitchen goes quiet, the only noise coming from the clock on the wall. I look back and forth between Mom and Dad, willing them to understand. One look at April tells me she's doing the same.

"I'll be honest," Dad says at last, "you've caught me a bit off guard, so I'm not exactly sure what to say. But I'm sorry if we've made you feel like you have to be in the middle of our, erm, *arguments*."

"So am I," Mom says quietly.

Dad sinks into a chair at the kitchen table and rubs his eyes. "As for working at the store, I don't see how we can change that right away, but we'll discuss it."

"What about Stanford, though?" April asks. "Are you seriously not going to let her go?"

Mom stiffens. "We can't be expected to change our minds at the last second just because the two of you decide to join forces, April. It's completely unreasonable."

"But you've known I wanted to go for *months*," I say. "You knew when I applied, and you knew when I got in. The only reason you said no—"

"Was because we needed your help!" Dad says. "The store can't stay afloat without you."

"Are you really talking about the store?" April asks. "Or about your marriage?"

The kitchen goes dead silent.

I'm immediately struck by the urge to tell Mom and Dad that April is kidding, that we know they only want me to stay in LA because it's what's best for the store, and by extension, our family. But I won't undermine April's bravery by running from the truth in her words.

I do have to say something, though.

"I've been working toward this for years," I say, "and I've been preparing to leave for months. I've got a dorm and my classes picked out and everything. I'm even packed, for the most part. The only thing that's left for me to do is to *go*."

"And to pay the rest of your expenses," Dad says.

"Right," I say. "I can't make you help if you don't want to."

Beside me, April's shoulders droop. "This is so unfair," she says. "Jenn's been working at the store for free for *years*. Can you imagine how much money she'd have saved up if you'd paid her?"

They start to argue about how it's a family business and you don't pay family, but I'm too busy doing the math in my head to pay attention. "Hold on," I say. "She's right."

Dad opens his mouth to protest, but I hold up my hand. "Not about you guys paying me," I explain, "about me being paid in general." I hop off the stool and start to pace back and forth across the kitchen. I'm so used to *not* being paid that it never occurred to me, but I've been working twenty hours a week for the last two and a half years. If I can keep that up at a job that pays *better* than minimum wage, I can probably cover the difference by myself. I stop pacing and look at Mom and Dad. "If I get a job, I won't need your help."

Mom looks alarmed. "But—but what about the store? I know you think we wouldn't need the extra help if your father and I . . . *handled* . . . things differently, but we can't be there twelve hours a day." She looks to Dad, and when she speaks again, she doesn't sound worried. She sounds hopeless. "I don't see how we would manage on our own."

"I'll do it," April says suddenly. "I'll work in the store after school and on the weekends. I'll pick up all of Jenn's shifts if I have to."

"April, no," I say. "You don't have to do that."

"Apparently, I do."

I turn to Mom and Dad, expecting to find a combined look of relief and doubt on their faces. But instead, they look . . . sad.

"You'd really do that?" Mom asks. "Even though you'd have to give up soccer?"

"Yes," April says. "I'd give it up if that means you can keep the store open." She smiles sadly at me. "It's my turn to help."

Mom crosses the kitchen and wraps her arms around April. "Thank you, sweetheart."

April's eyes fill with tears. "You're welcome," she chokes out.

"You can't do this," I say, shaking my head. "April, tell them about USC. *Tell them.*"

April grimaces. "Jenn, it's fine."

"It's *not* fine," I say, turning to Mom and Dad. "Did you guys know that April is on the varsity team this year? And that she's so good that USC is interested in her?"

Dad looks to April. "Really?"

"Yes, *really*," she says. "A USC rep is coming to watch me play. They could give me a scholarship for college."

"Isn't that awesome?" I beam at my sister. I did a shitty job of supporting her when she told me about the scholarship in the car. I'm not going to make that mistake again.

"Hold on," Dad says. "How likely is this? It just seems like they're going to be really picky about who they recommend."

"They are," she says.

"How do you know they'll pick you, then?" Mom asks softly. "Or that USC will decide to offer a scholarship?"

April lifts her chin, but instead of looking stubborn, she looks strong. "I don't know for sure," she says. "But I *do* know I'm good at this, and that I work hard. I have a shot."

"But only if she's on the team," I add. "If she's not, the USC rep will never see her. No team, no USC."

"And you can't be on the team if you miss games," Mom says quietly.

"Or practices," April adds. "I've got to be all in, or I'm out."

Mom and Dad look at each other for the first time since April called them out. I half expect them to start arguing again, but instead they stare at each other for a long time, communicating in that silent way they used to do all the time when we were kids. "A scholarship is a big deal," Dad says at last. "We wouldn't want you to miss out on the chance at getting one."

"No," Mom agrees. "We wouldn't."

They share another long look, then Mom reaches out and gently tugs one of April's curls. "I think it might be time we tried running the store on our own. At least for a little while."

"Oh, thank god," April says, sagging back in her seat. "I really didn't want to work there."

Mom barks out a laugh, then covers her mouth.

"Wait," I say, barely daring to hope. "If we're not going to work at the store anymore, does that mean you're okay with me going?" I realize it sounds like I'm asking for permission, and I clarify quickly. "I mean, I'm going no matter what. But I'd feel a lot better if you guys were on board."

Dad crosses his arms and fixes me with a look he once reserved for misbehaving employees. "Do you really think you can work a part-time job *and* keep your grades up?"

I take a page out of April's book and lift my chin. "Yes."

He watches me a second longer, then gives me a curt nod. "Then I'm on board."

I turn slowly to Mom, afraid of what I'll find when I look at her. "Mom?"

She picks up the tomato again and rolls it slowly back and forth along the counter with her palm. "You said you're not finished packing," she says at last. "I suppose I better help."

My eyes fill with tears. It's not exactly her blessing, but it's still an olive branch. I grab it without hesitation. "Yes, please."

Mom puts down the tomato and wraps me in a tight hug. "I love you, Jelly Belly," she whispers.

I laugh into her shoulder. I still hate that nickname, but not everything is going to change overnight. "I love you too."

"We are going to have a serious talk once you're settled in," Mom says when she eventually pulls away. "In fact," she says, looking to Dad, "we should see if any tickets to San Francisco are still available for tomorrow. We might be able to find a deal—"

"I have another idea," I say. "What if April comes with me instead?"

April's eyes widen. "You want me to go to college with you?"

"Just for a night or two. We could take a mini road trip, and you could drive back on your own." The weight of the request hits me before the words are out of my mouth. Things are better between us, but this is still a big ask. "If you want to, I mean."

"Are you kidding?" April says. "I'd love to!" She throws her arms around me in a tight hug. When she pulls back, she's grinning. "And not just because this means I get to keep the car."

I roll my eyes, but I can't help smiling. "You're the worst."

CHAPTER 33

APRIL

re you in there?" I whisper-shout through Nate's partly open window. I'm balanced on the bough of the oak tree that stands between our houses. Every time the wind blows, I picture falling to my death, and let me tell you—it isn't pretty. "Either way, I'm coming in."

I shove the window open, then carefully stretch one leg inside and scoot my way across. I've done this a million times, but this is the first time since we were kids. It's also the first time I've done it since I was more than four foot ten and one hundred pounds, and it turns out this window is kind of a tight fit.

I step into his room and straighten up just as Nate comes in . . . shirtless.

"What are you doing here?" he asks, spinning to close his door. "My mom will kill me if she catches you."

I drag my gaze away from his chest—when did Nate get

so cut?—and assume what I hope is a totally relaxed stance. "I wanted to talk to you, and the phone felt passé."

Nate laughs and gestures for me to take a seat on his bed. I do, but the moment my butt hits the sheets I'm filled with visions of all the things he's probably—definitely—done here with other girls, followed by the things that we might do here—and I stand up again.

"Everything okay?" he asks, quirking an eyebrow.

"Um, yeah," I say. "It's just, uh, you changed your sheets."

"Once a week, thank you very much."

I laugh. "I meant you don't have the same sheets you did when we were kids. All your sheets were—"

"Superheroes, yeah," he says, smiling. "They got washed so many times I stopped being able to tell the Spider-Man set and the Wonder Woman set apart, so I decided to get new ones. But don't worry—I still have them."

"Thank goodness."

We stare at each other from across the room, and suddenly I'm sweating. Why is he so quiet? Should I say something? Is he as nervous as I am? Does he regret kissing me? What if this whole thing between us was a mistake, and now our friendship is screwed up? How will we go back to the way things were? How will we—

"April," Nate says. "Come here."

I start toward him, but before I'm even a few steps across the room, Nate is there, his warm arms wrapped around my waist, his bare chest pressed against me. "Everything is fine," he says, reading my mind like he always has. "Better than fine, actually."

"Are you sure?" I ask. "Because if you're regretting what happened, we can always—"

He dips his head and presses his lips to mine. It's sweet and soft, and the tenseness in my shoulders melts away. This is nothing like kissing Eric. There's no nervousness, no worry. It's just me and Nate, like always.

Then he lifts me up and carries me to the bed, and it's still me and Nate, but not like always—it's totally new, and totally *hot*. I wrap my legs around him as the kiss deepens and intensifies, and soon I'm not thinking about anything at all. When he eventually pulls back, I feel drunk with happiness.

I smile. "That was—"

"Yeah."

"We should do it more often—"

"Yeah."

"Can I have a million dollars?"

"Wait—what?"

"Nothing," I say, shrugging. "Just wanted to make sure you were paying attention."

He laughs, and then suddenly we're both cracking up, then shushing each other, then cracking up again. We also do a bit more kissing, followed by even more laughing.

"Oh god, you're going to get me in so much trouble," Nate says when we've both finally calmed down enough to catch our breath. He leans over and kisses me gently. "By the way, I forgot to ask. How did it go with your parents?"

"Really well," I say, brushing my nose against his. "They're on board with Jenn going to Stanford. They won't help her pay the rest of her expenses—not this year, anyway—but she's going to get a job. If anyone can balance school and a part-time gig, it's Jenn."

"That's great," he says, pulling me up so we can sit side by side. "And what about you? Are you going to be the newest employee at the esteemed O'Farrell Antiques?"

"Sorry to disappoint," I say, shaking my head. "But they're going to try to make it work without me. Actually, Jenn told them about how the fighting is affecting the store, and they're going to work on that too."

"That's incredible," he says. "Do you think it'll actually work?"

"I don't know," I say. "I hope so."

"Me too."

He pulls me toward him, and before I know it I'm on top of him, straddling his hips as his hands wander my body. If kissing him felt hot before, this feels positively on fire. "I want you," I say into his mouth as he kisses me. "I'm not trying to rush you, but—"

"You're not," he says. "But I promised I would—"

His phone buzzes on his desk.

"—talk to my brother."

"Is that him?" I ask, sitting up.

He nods and grabs the phone, then comes back to the bed. "I can call him back," he says as the phone buzzes again. "It's going to be awkward anyway, and it's late—"

"Don't you dare." I stand, then take an extra step away from the bed for good measure. "I want you to talk to him."

"Are you sure?"

The phone buzzes a third time. "Yes. Call me tomorrow?"

"Tonight," he says as he accepts the call. "I'll call you tonight."

I give him a quick kiss, then push open his window. It's a slow climb down, and an even slower climb through the window into the downstairs bathroom of my house. By the time I step out into the hallway, cool as can be, there's a text waiting for me.

We're still on the phone, Nate says. **Bo asked who I was talking to when I picked up. I told him it was you and that we're dating now. He said "about time."**

Damn right, I type back.

I hurry up the stairs and stop outside Jenn's door. Music is playing softly, and I can hear the murmur of her talking to someone on the phone. For once I decide not to listen in, and instead I continue to my room and lie down on my bed. But before I can get comfortable, there's a knock on the door.

"Come in," I call.

Jenn slips inside and closes the door behind her. "That was Grandma. I told her I'm going to Stanford."

I scoot over in bed, and she sits beside me. Her hair is wet and already starting to curl. It looks just like mine does when I get out of the shower.

"Was she happy?" I ask as she puts her feet under the covers and lies down.

"Yes. We're going to have lunch next week."

"And what about Thomas? Did you call him, too?"

"We texted."

"How did it go? Did you get back together?"

"No," she says. "I told him how it went with Mom and Dad, and that I'm not going to be flying up with him tomorrow." She rests her head on my shoulder, her wet curls cool against my neck. "I'm really happy you're coming with me instead."

"Me too."

I close my eyes and listen to my sister's breathing slow beside me as she falls asleep. This entire day feels like it was a dream. The Ferris wheel. The man lifting Jenn onto his shoulders. The chill of the water as I tumbled into the canal. The fight we had in the car. Some of it still hurts, but in a distant way, like it happened to someone else. Or maybe like it happened to me, but a different me.

Either way, today was a good day. And if the way it ended is any indication, tomorrow is going to be even better.

Acknowledgments

Thank you to my wonderful agent, Jim McCarthy, who always gives it to me straight, and to my editor, Catherine Laudone, who is endlessly patient even when my first draft has so many ellipses and em dashes that my book looks like it was written in Morse code. Thank you also to the wonderful marketing and publicity folks at Simon & Schuster, and to my brilliant cover designer, Krista Vossen, for giving me the cover of my teen self's dreams. You knocked it out of the park.

I'm also very grateful to my brilliant critique partners, Juliana L. Brandt, Bess Cozby, Hannah Fergesen, Elizabeth Lim, and Rachel Lynn Solomon. You guys helped me make this book what I wanted it to be, and I am eternally grateful.

Thank you also to the Electric 18s, who continue to be a source of comfort and joy, and to the Highlights Foundation. Cabin 16 is my home away from home.

I'd also like to acknowledge the incredibly important and often thankless work that librarians, booksellers, and book-peddling teachers do every single day. You guys are superheroes, and on behalf of authors (and readers!) everywhere, *thank you.*

I could not have written this book without the support of my family. I am lucky to have the encouragement of not only my dad, grandma, godmother Gail, uncle Mark, and extended family, but also my best friends in the entire universe—my husband, Patrick, and my sister, Diana. Jenn and April might be the worst, but you two are the best.

Finally, I'd like to thank readers for giving my books a chance. I couldn't live this dream without you.